DEAD MAN'S CANYON

After the Civil War, former ranger Nicolas Kilpatrick and his fellow ex-soldiers continue to deploy their skills, protecting settlers from Indian attacks and tracking down gangs of robbers and rustlers. In the wake of a shootout with the murderous Maitland Guerrillas, a dying bandit offers Nick information on the gang's leader — in exchange for a promise that his soon-to-be-widow will be taken care of. Setting off to chase down Frank Maitland and keep his vow, Nick heads out to Laramie . . .

Books by Terrell L. Bowers
in the Linford Western Library:

TERRELL L. BOWERS

◆

DEAD MAN'S CANYON

Complete and Unabridged

LINFORD
Leicester

First published in Great Britain in 2014 by
Robert Hale Limited
London

First Linford Edition
published 2016
by arrangement with
Robert Hale Limited
London

A catalogue record for this book is available
from the British Library.

ISBN 978–1–4448–2858–0

Published by
F. A. Thorpe (Publishing)
Anstey, Leicestershire

Set by Words & Graphics Ltd.
Anstey, Leicestershire
Printed and bound in Great Britain by
T. J. International Ltd., Padstow, Cornwall

This book is printed on acid-free paper

For the wonderful new life who brings sunshine, joy and love into our lives . . . our granddaughter, Janessa Lynn Nicolodemos

1

Nicolas Kilpatrick rode into the massive yard of the north-eastern Colorado cattle ranch, intent upon seeing if Erwin Delatorre was hiring. He pulled his mount up short at the bizarre scene that unfolded before his eyes.

A slender young man was squared off against an older gent and three others who looked to be in their early- to mid-twenties. Any one of the four was half again the size of the smaller fellow.

'My daughter ain't gonna run with a no-account like you!' the elderly man bellowed, his face blazing red with rage. 'She's only fifteen!'

'She claimed to be older,' the youngster fired back haughtily. 'It ain't my fault if you don't raise your kids to tell the truth.'

'I'm gonna horsewhip you, sonny boy!' the father continued to rant. 'I'll

1

teach you to lay your dirty paws on an innocent girl.'

'Might be worth taking a few licks,' the joker cracked wise again. ''Cause that gal of yours sure learned to kiss from someone!'

'Why, you smart-mouthed . . . ' the father cried. 'Get him, boys!'

At his order the three who had not spoken up during the confrontation went after the youngster. The skinny kid was quick, ducking away from one, kicking another on the shin and diving between the legs of the third to upend him. The mad scramble stirred up a cloud of dust and no one could get a firm grasp on the slippery joker. He might have kept them falling over one another and grabbing at the air, except Papa jumped in and caught the elusive youth from behind.

The kid was game. He stomped down on Big Papa's foot with the heel of his boot, bringing a howl from the man's throat. He almost broke free, the elder statesman being momentarily hobbled from the pain, but two of the others quickly grabbed hold of each of his arms. The elusive young man was caught.

'Get the whip from the freight wagon!' Papa bellowed at the one boy not helping to restrain the joker. Then to his other two boys, 'Bind this sneaky coyote to the corral gate. I'm going to peel the hide right off of his bones!'

The brutal punishment sounded excessive, so Nick decided to intervene. He rode forward and everyone stopped what they were doing. He reined up a few feet away from the four of them and rested his hand on his Colt. Regarding the bunch with a frosty expression, he spoke with a cold authority.

'I have to take exception to using a bullwhip on the boy for kissing your daughter, mister,' he said. 'A lashing like that would likely cut a skinny kid like him in half.'

'Who the hell are you?' the old man

growled. 'And what gives you the right to interfere with what I aim to do to this young pup?'

'Name's Kilpatrick,' he answered. 'I came here to ask about a job.'

'That's me — Delatorre, owner of this ranch.' The man snorted his contempt. 'And you've got a peculiar way of asking for a job, challenging me on my own property.'

'Well, right is right, no matter who you are,' Nick told him easily. 'I understand my putting a stop to your dealing out punishment pretty well eliminates any chance of going to work for you.' He hardened his look and voice. 'I reckon I'd be even less welcome if I have to shoot you or one of your boys to prove I'm serious about what I say.'

None of the four men was armed. After a long moment's contemplation, Delatorre glowered at the boy. 'You get off of my land, you sneaky little weasel. If you ever come near my girl again, I'll string you up by your heels and let the coyotes and crows eat you alive.'

The kid flashed a smug grin. 'I'm not one to take advantage of a girl who ain't courting age, Pop. Maybe I'll check back with your girl in a couple years.'

'Ride out while you still can, you insolent whippersnapper!' Delatorre roared. 'And don't come back.'

The boy retrieved his horse and joined Nick. The two of them headed back in the direction of Denver. Nick rode at a lope for the first mile . . . just in case the Delatorre family decided to grab their guns and come after them. Once satisfied there was no pursuit, he slowed to a walk and took a closer look at the young man.

'You don't seem to put much store in your own life, fella.'

'Jeremiah Chamberlin is the name,' the youth told him, ignoring his comment. 'Most folks call me JC. It saves time.'

Nick introduced himself, asked JC his age, and surveyed the young man. He was a young-looking eighteen, with

5

a stage actor's good looks. He had wavy brown hair and bright brown eyes, was three or four inches shorter than Nick's five foot ten inches and probably weighed in at about a hundred and twenty pounds.

'You didn't have to butt in,' JC informed him after a time. 'I coulda handled them.'

'I noticed how, by being one step away from a severe whipping, you were luring them into overconfidence.'

The boy grinned. It was an infectious smile, part mischief and part humor, as if he found life a combination of entertainment and challenge.

'Where do you live?'

'I have a job in town,' JC answered. 'Working at the livery. I tend the animals and also make deliveries for some of the stores. Sometimes I drive the stage for the express office too.' He shrugged his shoulders. 'That's how I met up with Ellie Mae.' He heaved a deep sigh. 'Man, I really did think she was a year or two older.'

'Have you been working for the livery long?'

'Since I was left on my own about three years back. It don't pay much, but a man has to do what he can to survive.'

'No argument from me,' Nick returned. 'I'm between jobs myself.'

'I suppose you're going to blame me for ruining any shot you had at going to work for Delatorre?'

Nick smiled at the humor in the boy's delivery. 'My only question is . . . was the girl worth all of the trouble?'

JC whistled his satisfaction. 'I got to tell you, Nick. By the time Ellie Mae is full grown, every man between Denver and Cheyenne is going to be panting at her heels.'

Nick laughed. 'Wish I'd have gotten a look at her. It would have kept my trip from being a complete waste of time.'

Even as they were joking back and forth a fast-moving rider appeared on the trail ahead. Nick was surprised to see that the man on horseback was Gus

Gaston, a man he knew well. They stopped while Gus continued running his mount until he was close enough to recognize Nick. Then he pulled up his laboring horse and let the animal blow.

'Glad I didn't have to go all the way to the Delatorre ranch to find you, Captain.'

'What's up, Gus?'

'A band of outlaws held up the bank over in Golden. The police are short-handed and desperate for a posse. I happened to be in town buying supplies and the mayor asked for our help.'

'*Our* help?'

'There were four bandits — three of them known killers. The mayor offered a handsome reward if we can get back the money and bring them in.'

'Be a chore for just the two of us.'

'Three,' interjected JC. 'I'm game.'

Nick ignored the kid as Gus added: 'The Simmons boys and Loudermilk are in Denver. I can have them ready to ride in an hour.'

'What are we waiting for?' JC

8

declared. 'Let's go drag those mangy dogs back to a prison cell.'

'I don't remember inviting you,' Nick spoke to JC.

The boy grinned. 'You'll soon find that I don't require much encouragement to join in a good fight. And if there's money to be made, you ain't gonna keep me away.'

Nick did what came natural to him: he took charge. 'All right. You two ride back to Denver. Round up the others and pick up supplies enough for a few days. I'll head over to Golden, talk to the mayor and pick up the bandits' trail. Get yourselves fresh horses and we'll all meet at the creek crossing.'

Gus gave a nod. Nick whirled about and rode off at a gallop.

JC stuck out his hand to Gus. The man hesitated a moment, then took it in a short shake. Turning his horse back toward Denver, he announced: 'Welcome to Kilpatrick's Rangers!'

JC stuck at his side and raised his

eyebrows in puzzlement. 'Kilpatrick's Rangers?'

The two of them started moving at an easy pace and Gus explained. 'It's a brand we earned during the war,' he said. 'Kilpatrick is wily as a fox and takes command without thinking. He and some of us entered the war when Colorado became a territory back in '61. By the time the Confederacy surrendered Kilpatrick was a captain and commanded a special fighting force — they called us rangers.

'We weren't attached to any one unit but did a lot of independent raiding on our own, usually hitting supply trains or keeping tabs on troop movements and hunting down small guerilla bands.'

'The war's been over for several years,' JC said.

'Yes, but when we returned to Colorado there was Indian trouble waiting. Kilpatrick and some of us volunteered to help protect the outlying farms and ranches from attack. We continued to act as rangers, chasing renegades and battling with raiding parties until the four tribes — Cheyenne, Arapaho, Kiowa and Comanche — were settled in Oklahoma.'

'That's why this mayor trusts Kilpatrick to hunt down these outlaws?'

'Yep. We did more good than the army when it came to stopping the local Indian raids. The army often sent troops, but they weren't trained for this kind of warfare and moved too slowly. By the time they reacted to an attack the Indians were long gone. We were on their trail within a matter of hours and tracked a good many of them down.'

'So these other men we're going to pick up, they are ex-rangers too?'

'Best in the country. Andy and John Simmons are both excellent marksmen and Bob Loudermilk is a tracking fool.' He shot the new kid a grin. 'We'll nab those bandits before the week is out.'

2

Roughly one hundred miles away another group that had been active during the war arrived at the thriving mining community of Leadville, Colorado. However, these men had been on the opposite side from Kilpatrick and his rangers.

When the war broke out between the Union and the Confederacy Frank Maitland saw it as an opportunity to benefit from his family's shady line of work. He was the eldest of four brothers and they quickly offered to join with the South and fight. However, the term *join* was not indicative of how the Maitland gang waged war.

While William Quantrill led the biggest and most notorious of the guerilla bands, there were others. Jeb Stewart, Nathaniel Bedford Forrest, and the Reynolds gang from Texas also raided and plundered throughout the country in the name of the Confederacy. Adding a dozen or so strays to his own band, the Maitland Guerillas did the same. Wearing uniforms of gray, they stole, pillaged and robbed throughout the country, all under the guise of helping the South.

Of course, like most Rebel bands at that time, they gave exactly nothing to the Confederacy . . . except, perhaps, a bad name. The Maitland Guerillas ventured as far as New Mexico, but that was a desolate territory and the distances between potential targets were too great, so they looted and robbed mostly around Colorado and Kansas. Many men joined or left during the long and bitter war, but a few stayed loyal to Frank and his gang. In the years following the war's end the robberies and attacks became more risky. The outlaws had to evade not only the posse from any nearby town, but also Union soldiers, who came to occupy the forts in an effort to squash the Indian raids.

This was their first visit to Leadville and Frank happened to run into an old acquaintance. Lex Bishop had been a part of Frank's Rebel group for three years, but had taken his ill-gotten gains and left the gang shortly before the war ended. The two men both happened to meet at the bar counter to get drinks at the same time. Otherwise they might have missed seeing each other.

'Hot-damn, Bishop!' Frank greeted him warmly. 'Been a coon's age since I set eyes on you. How are you doing?'

Lex gave him a firm handshake. 'Frank, you old buzzard! It's been a few seasons at that.'

Frank laughed. 'Who you calling old? If I remember right, you're only a year younger than me.'

'Yeah, but I'm young at heart. It makes all the difference.'

'Come join us at the table,' Frank offered. 'Dan and Ken are here too.'

Lex followed Frank as he threaded his way between the tables in the crowded room. Two of Frank's brothers, Dan and Ken, called a greeting to him before he had a chance to sit down.

'What are you boys doing in this mining town?' Lex wanted to know. 'You're not thinking of digging ore for a living or hauling freight, are you?'

The trio laughed at the idea. 'No way,' said Ken. 'Never,' added Dan. Frank simply gave his head a negative shake.

'How about you, Lex?' Ken asked. 'Are you living here?'

Lex sobered at once. 'I've been dealing faro at one of the saloons. It don't pay squat, but I ran out of money a few months back and had to find me a job. I've got a wife now, with a kid on the way.'

'Aw, no! Say it ain't so.' Frank guffawed his amazement. 'Why would an old stag like you want to do something that dumb?'

Lex gave a solemn shake of his head. 'I reckon I was plumb out of my mind, Frank. I started flirting with a little filly who was working at a laundry, and the next thing I knew, she was dragging me in front of a parson.'

'I warned you to stay away from that rotgut whiskey!' Ken jeered.

'Yeah, you should know hard liquor and sweet-talking women don't mix for shucks,' Dan contributed.

Lex rubbed his temples on both sides, as if he had a major headache. 'I never felt so trapped in my life, boys. If the girl wasn't in the family way, I'd pack up and sneak out on her in the middle of the night.'

'Spoken like the honorable gentleman you are,' Frank teased.

Lex chuckled and looked around. 'Where's the kid?'

Frank knew he was speaking of the youngest member of the family. 'He's outside town at our camp, him and a couple of others — you remember Skye and Gato, don't you?'

'Sure, they were around when I was riding with you.' Lex recalled that Skye's mother was a Ute Indian and

Gato had fled from Mexico with a price on his head. 'What kind of deal have you got going that you need extra men?'

Dan answered with a smirk. 'It's the same kind of work we did for the Confederacy . . . except we don't have to wear the gray uniforms.'

Lex looked at both Ken and Frank. At their nods, he knew they weren't stringing him along. His face flashed with a stark realization. 'Oh, yeah! I've heard about an ex-Rebel gang raiding throughout the country; I just never thought about it being you. I figured you would have pulled stakes and gone straight after the war ended.'

Frank punched him in the arm. 'Ain't no money in running a small ranch.'

'Even when you rustle the cattle,' Dan added with a grin.

Ken also smirked. 'Yeah, this pays a lot better and we don't have to break our backs working sixty hours a week.'

'I can tell you from experience, that's not a lot of fun,' Lex confirmed. 'I'm sure tired of busting my hump, slaving away for someone else, and going home broke every night.'

'Mayhap we can help one another out.'

'I'm listening,' Lex replied. 'What have you got in mind?'

Frank lowered his voice and leaned over closer. 'What do you know about the handling of the local payrolls? We're looking for a place we can hit without a lot of risk, something with a fair-sized wad of cash and little chance of being caught.'

Lex did some contemplation before he answered. 'If I help you, I want back in the gang. Are there only the six of you?'

'For this job,' Dan informed him. 'When we need the manpower, we've got ten to fifteen.' With a wink, 'However, we can always use an able man like yourself.'

'Sounds promising.'

'We'll find a spot for you and do you a favor to boot,' Frank said. Lex leaned in closer, the interest keen in his eyes, and listened.

'You help us with our little chore here in town,' Frank continued, 'and you and your wife can stay at our ranch.'

'I thought you said there was no money in ranching?'

'We needed a regular place to hole up between jobs,' Ken explained, 'so we bought a rundown cow spread across the Wyoming border. Ain't put a lot of money into the place, because we only use it for a home between jobs. Even so, there's an old line shack a ways from the main house that's sitting empty. You and your wife could have it as your own. You'd have a place to live and still be handy whenever we went out to do a job.'

'That would be great,' Lex said enthusiastically.

Ken looked around, making sure no one was listening, then asked: 'So tell us, how do we get the most out of a single robbery?'

Lex smiled. 'The mine payrolls are

too well guarded. The last bunch who tried a robbery ended up buried in the local graveyard. However, early Sunday morning would be a good time to hit the place where I work. There isn't anyone around except for one guard and the two people who count and put away the money. I've gone in a time or two when my table closed late. Saturday is payday, so they will have several thousand dollars on hand. They will open the door for me. We tie them up, grab the money and we're gone.'

Frank stuck out his hand. 'Tell your wife to get packed and ready to move, Lex. Come Sunday morning, you're leaving with us!'

★   ★   ★

The four bank robbers were holed up inside a farmhouse. As the sun began to dip over the western horizon, Nicolas Kilpatrick, JC and the four ex-rangers were in position to see the body of one man lying out in the middle of the yard.

An overturned bucket was a few feet away and the victim was clad in bib-overalls and a worn straw hat.

'Dirty lowdown skunks!' JC grated through clenched teeth. 'Kilt that innocent farmer and likely got the rest of the family inside.'

'The Bensons,' Bob chipped in. 'I spent a night here during a snowstorm once. There were two grown men — brothers, along with a woman and a couple of kids.'

Careful to stay hidden from sight, Nick and his men watched for movement about the yard. When a man showed himself Bob identified him as the husband and father. He was about forty years of age. Gray hair showed in his moustache and about his ears from under a worn, floppy hat, and his back was bowed from his many years of working the fields. He tended to the stock and then milked the lone milk cow. When finished with the chores, he paused a moment to stare down at his dead brother, then solemnly returned to the house. It was nearly dusk when a lamp came to life inside. With curtains drawn over the windows, only a couple of vague shadows were distinguishable whenever anyone moved around inside.

'What's the plan?' JC was growing anxious. 'We make any move against those four killers and they will sure 'nuff use the woman and kids to trade for their freedom.'

Nick responded thoughtfully. 'They seem to think they are safe for the night.'

'No guard posted,' Gus agreed. 'That suggests confidence bordering on stupidity.'

Nick studied the layout from their position of concealment among the brushy hillock, a good fifty yards away. Turning over ideas in his head, he outlined the situation aloud to the others.

'According to the mayor, the gang is led by Dirty Carter. The others are Kid-Gloves Gore, Ferret Clinton and a fourth unknown gunman. They have to suppose that a posse is on their back trail, but obviously don't expect company tonight. Bob recognized their attempt to make a false trail and cover their tracks. He got us here quicker than anyone else in the country could have.'

'Reckon they'll hole up here for the night and move on in the morning, Captain,' Gus surmised. 'There's a chance they won't feel the family is a threat to them, so they'll leave them be.'

'They sure enough killed the one old gent,' JC growled. 'We can't trust them not to murder the whole family.'

'We'll wait until full dark before we make our move,' Nick said, having formulated a plan that might work.

'You're the boss,' Andy whispered. 'You call the tune and we will sure enough dance to it.'

'Put the horses down the hill where there's no chance they will be heard if one of them decides to whinny some. Then everyone get something to eat. No fire and no noise. We don't want to give up the advantage of surprise.'

The men hurried to follow his orders. Nick was aware of their movements, but he kept watch over the house below. He felt the familiar pang in his gut, the worry of command. How many times had he led his men into battle or on a raid? A dozen encounters with Johnny Rebs and even more with Indian war parties or renegades. He worried his luck would run out, that he'd make a mistake and would get everyone killed.

Even as he watched the dying light in the dusk he remembered the faces and names of those who had been wounded or died while under his command. He was responsible for each man's life. A death haunted his dreams at night and often invaded his thoughts during the day. Telling himself that someone had to make the hard choices didn't help to pacify his conscience.

'You got a plan for nabbing those coyotes without them killing the family inside the house yet?' JC asked quietly, shocking his brain back to their present situation.

'Maybe,' Nick answered. 'They still haven't posted a guard outside.'

'That's good, ain't it?'

Nick took a second look at the youthful volunteer. No bigger than he was, he might be able to do something that he and the others could not. 'It allows us to make a move that might prevent anyone from getting killed.'

'Yeah?' The kid's expression brightened. 'We going to surround the house and make noise like there are a hundred of us and trick them into surrendering?'

'I was thinking of something a little more cunning than that. If the plan works, we will take them all alive and without much of a fight.'

JC's eyes widened. 'You're joshing me. How can we take them without a fight?'

Nick pinned him with a hard look. 'I said without *much* of a fight,' he clarified.

'OK, Kilpatrick,' JC said, displaying a

25

grin. 'Your pals in arms have been bragging to me how smart you are about setting an ambush, so I'll follow your lead.' His features morphed into his carefree simper. 'But I got to tell you, I could have handled this on my own.'

3

Nick and his men found what they needed in the barn. Sticking to the dark shadows, they moved to the side of the house. The Simmons boys crawled to the front porch dragging along a bucket, while Nick and JC selected a stealthy access to one corner of the roof. JC had a thick old piece of canvas draped over his shoulder.

'Slow and gentle,' Nick cautioned. 'Stay on the crossbeams.'

JC grinned. 'I'll move as light as a spider, Fearless Leader. Don't worry, I won't knock any dirt loose from the rafters to alert the killers.'

Nick patted him on the shoulder, assumed a squatting position and cupped his hands for a foothold. JC felt as light as a child as Nick lifted him up on to the roof.

JC proceeded slowly and carefully until

he reached the chimney. Then he used the canvas to cover the opening. From the amount of smoke and what they had overheard from a window below, the farmer's wife was in the process of cooking supper for everyone. That chore was going to take a nasty turn.

Easing back down from the roof, Nick helped JC down and then took up a position near a window. Andy had quietly wedged a post against the back door, blocking it shut. He remained to keep watch there while JC and the other three men got ready at the front. Everything was in place.

'What the . . . ?' a husky voice snarled from inside. 'What did you do to the stove, woman?'

Before she could answer, one of the other men coughed. 'Hey! The whole place is filling up with smoke. She must've closed the damper!'

'No!' the woman cried. 'I didn't do anything! Something must have fallen into the chimney. That happened once last winter.'

'Open the windows and air the place out!' came the order from one of the men.

Nick stood out of sight as one of the men jerked open the window. However, the smoke was filling the room faster than it could vent through the lone opening. A couple people in the room began to cough and choke.

'I'm dying here!' a new man's voice resonated angrily. 'I'll go check up on the roof. Maybe I can see what's going on.'

'I'm outa here too,' voiced another man. 'Smoke is getting so thick you can't see across the room!'

Two men came out the door and both of them slipped on the greased porch and fell. Before they could get to their feet, a third man blindly stumbled out and toppled over them, landing on one's head and the other's legs.

'Ow!' yelped one. 'Watch it, Ferret.'

'Quit your steppin' on me,' cried the other.

The posse moved in at once, guns

drawn, and quickly covered the three men. Nick peeked through the window. When Kid-Gloves Gore heard what was happening, he made a grab for the woman. Her husband moved quickly to protect her, but Gore punched him in the jaw, knocking him down. The farmer's intervention allowed enough time for Nick to climb through the window. He had Gore under his gun at once.

'Stand where you are or you're dead!' he commanded.

Gore had caught hold of one of the woman's arms, but there was no chance for him to pull his pistol. He rubbed his watering eyes, uttered a sigh of defeat and released her. The woman quickly gathered up her children and helped her husband out of the smoke-filled house. Gore stood with a sneer on his lips, blinked against the acrid haze, and shook his head.

'I should have guessed someone had messed with the chimney. Who the hell are you?'

'I'm one of the men who is going to take you to jail, Gore. You and your men have robbed your last bank.'

The bandit looked outside to see his three men were already prisoners and swore vehemently. 'You're a bunch of yella', slinkin' coyotes. I should have put a man outside as lookout.'

'What you should have done is not rob and kill people for a living. I'll take a special interest in watching you being hanged or hauled away in a prison wagon.'

★   ★ ★

The excitement of having a place of their own was quickly dampened for Darlene Bishop. Their new *home* was a rundown, one-room shanty, a couple miles away from the main ranch, and it quickly became more of a prison than a home. Darlene spent the bulk of her time cleaning the house and serving meals to Lex, whenever he chose to come home. She did all of the household chores, cut wood for the fireplace and foraged for wild strawberries, currants and other berries. There was a stream a quarter-mile away, so she carried water to the house each day for drinking, cooking, washing and laundry. It was a lonely, laborious, thankless existence, and there was often little food in the house.

As for Lex, he frequently spent the money he earned gambling or drinking with the Maitland boys. Buying food was a low priority to him. However, he did take Darlene to buy supplies each month at the local trading post. It was about the only time she ever left the tiny hovel and she bought as much as Lex would allow. Even stocking up, she often ended up with bare cupboards and nothing to eat in the house before the next shopping trip. Several times, when the Maitlands were gone on one of their longer trips, she made the long walk to their house and scrounged enough food to keep from starving.

To worsen the situation, she discovered that the Maitlands were outlaws.

On the eve of an upcoming job, and having kept silent for several weeks, she confronted Lex.

'I know how we got our own home — if this old line shack can be called that. You helped rob the saloon before we left Leadville.'

Lex grimaced, then anchored his jaw with his teeth set firmly. 'I did what I did for our future, Darlene. It was for you and the kid.'

Reminded of the child growing inside of her, Darlene fought back tears of frustration. 'But I don't want our baby to grow up with a band of robbers and thieves. I don't want to see the father of my child being hauled off to prison or the gallows.'

'Look,' he snarled bitterly. 'I'm doing what I have to do. Dealing faro or tending bar isn't how I want to earn a living. I'm not cut out for that kind of life.'

'I heard Josh say there were a dozen more men over at Shady Cove, all ready to ride with the Maitlands, yet you go

33

out on every job? Why can't you stay home some of the time?'

She thought she knew Lex, but she had never seen such a cold, dark expression on his face, never felt such a bite of frost from his steely-cold glare. This was not the suave, debonair gentleman he had pretended to be when they met. This was a man capable of using his gun and shooting someone to get what he wanted.

'Because I'm the only one with a nagging wife and hungry brat on the way,' he vented harshly. 'None of the others have the expense and responsibility of a wife and house of their own. You just be happy to take care of this cabin and fix meals for me when I'm here.' He grated the words with cool deliberation. 'When the runt arrives, you can worry about tending to him as well. That's all you need to do.' With finality, 'As for me, I'll continue to ride on every job so we have enough money to keep a roof over our heads and have food on the table.'

'Josh Maitland caught me by the creek and tried to kiss me the other day,' Darlene blurted out. 'And when you were talking to Frank at the trading post last week, Dan pinched my bottom! These men don't respect you or me!'

Lex shrugged it off. 'The Maitland boys are a little crass in their playfulness, but they won't go too far as long as I'm around.'

'They treat me more like community property than a respectable wife. What will happen to me if you get hurt or killed while out stealing and terrorizing people for a living?'

'Give your jaw a rest,' he said, and sighed. 'You wanted out of your old life — well, here you are. Quit your bellyaching and make the best of it.'

Knowing any further debate was useless, Darlene stormed over and got into bed. As usual, Lex did not follow. He was off to spend the night with Frank and his brothers, drinking, playing cards, or planning the job ahead. As soon as he left the house, Darlene lay in the dark and reflected upon her hopeless situation.

'Lord,' she murmured reverently, 'I know I'm supposed to honor and obey my husband, but I don't want to raise my child among a pack of thieves and murderers. Please help me find a way out of this horrid situation.'

* * *

The town council was in agreement. Nick Kilpatrick and his ex-rangers had done a superb job. Even the governor had been impressed at the capture of four deadly gunmen without a shot being fired.

'We still have a sizeable border gang that must be dealt with,' the chairman announced.

The Denver mayor bobbed his head in agreement. 'They are a dangerous and wily bunch . . . Maitland's Guerillas,' he explained. 'They were a ruthless band of raiders during the war, using the Confederacy as an excuse for their looting and robberies. Once the war ended, they continued with their criminal ways. Over the years they have hit stage offices, banks, trading posts and travelers from here through Kansas, all the way to the New Mexico and Wyoming borders.'

'I've heard of them,' Nick replied. 'But I didn't know they ever came close to Denver.'

'They pick their targets, seem to have a pool of twenty or more men, and sometimes go into hiding for months at a time. A number of posses and even regular army troops have had no luck tracking them down.'

'They are going to keep pillaging, robbing and killing until they are stopped!' one businessman declared.

Nick displayed confusion. 'Me and the other rangers were disbanded when the Indian troubles ended. It's lucky there were several of us in town to go after Dirty Carter and the others.'

'We are aware of that, Mr Kilpatrick,'

the mayor contributed. 'However, we believe five or six men ought to be enough to do the job. Although Maitland sometimes shows up with a score of men, he seldom has more than eight or ten men with him during any one job. With the element of surprise . . . '

'The mayor's right,' the spokesman for the town council concurred. 'You and a handful of your rangers did a right thorough job of bringing in those bank robbers. And we're willing to pay wages for you and a few good men until the job is done. Plus, several banks and express companies are offering sizeable rewards for the Maitlands. That means a handsome bonus when this is finished.'

'You want to deputize us, is that it?' Nick asked.

'It's Kilpatrick's Rangers we need for one more job,' the spokesman said.

The mayor pounded his fist on the tabletop to drive home his point. 'These men have to be stopped. We will make it worth your while until you can locate and deal with these cowardly parasites.'

Nick gave the idea some thought. It seemed a good way to earn a stake while also doing service for that part of the country.

'One more job for the rangers, huh?'

'We will authorize you and those you pick to act in that capacity, a special force to deal with this band of murdering cutthroats.'

'I'll need a little money up front to fit out six men. I want every man armed with a new Winchester repeating rifle, and each will need a good horse.'

The mayor smiled. 'Whatever you need, Mr Kilpatrick. Whatever you need.'

★   ★   ★

Twice the Maitland Guerrillas had hit the stage to Canyon City when it was carrying a sizeable payment for the oil and kerosene produced there. Nick suspected one of the gang was being

39

tipped off about the transfer of money. Either that, or they intercepted the telegraph messages and determined when the cash payment was being sent. He secretly met with the stage and express line and proposed a way to protect the strongbox and capture or kill some of the gang. The owners jumped at the idea.

For the specified journey, passengers boarded the regular stage and the money was put into the strongbox. The stage pulled out on time and left town as usual. However, once the coach was a mile from town, the driver took a detour down to a shady cove and stopped alongside a creek. Nick and JC, along with the four ex-rangers, who had helped with the successful mission against Dirty Carter's gang, were waiting with a second coach. They continued along the route as a decoy. The passengers and regular stage allowed them an hour's head start and then resumed their trip.

JC, having had some experience

driving stage, managed the reins and guided the team. Nick rode shotgun at his side, with brothers Andy and John, plus Gus and Bob inside the coach.

'You think this is going to work?' JC asked, after a short way. 'I mean, this being a ranger is exciting and all, but I'd hate to get shot full of holes and have the plan fail miserably.'

'Why is everything about you, JC?' Nick teased. 'As long as they are shooting at you, the rest of us can return fire without worry of being hit.'

'Oh, you've a great way of lifting a guy's spirits,' JC grumbled. 'I'm sitting up here, the number one target for a bunch of outlaws, and it's supposed to make me happy?'

'You're the one who begged me for the chance to come along.'

'Yeah, but I joined for the big payday, so I'd have lots of money to spend. I didn't volunteer to become worm food on Boot Hill.'

'If you get shot full of holes, I'll see that you get the best funeral your share of the money can buy.'

'That makes everything all better,' JC grunted sourly.

'Elk's Point is just around the bend,' Nick warned. 'Better be ready to duck.'

'You ever try ducking while you're holding the reins to a team of horses?'

Before Nick had a chance to reply, three groups of four riders each appeared. One quartet spread across the trail on horseback, while another moved in from either side of the coach. JC pulled back on the reins, pretending he was going to slow the stage to a stop. Then, with a shout at the team, and a slap of the reins, he drove the horses forward at the men blocking the way.

Nick leveled the double-barrel shotgun, pulled one trigger and then the next. At the same time the four rangers inside the coach opened up with rifles.

Sporadic gunfire erupted from the startled bandits, but they were unprepared for the intense fire coming from the coach.

JC ducked low as Nick shoved the

shotgun down into the front boot and drew his Colt revolver. It was momentary mayhem, with men shouting and shooting, while their horses balked, spun about, and shied away from the explosive gunfire. Bullets chipped wood next to Nick, screaming past his ear, and he heard JC swear from being stung by a hastily fired round.

Several saddles were emptied, evidence of the deadly aim of the four marksmen from inside the coach. Nick's shotgun blasts had knocked one man from his horse and wounded one or two more. Using his handgun, he scored a third hit and the man sagged over his saddle and then sprawled on to the ground.

JC regained control of the team and pulled back on the reins as the bandits scattered for safety. Once the excited team slowed to a stop, Bob and those from inside the coach moved quickly to take charge of the men on the ground. Gus hurried over and checked each of the downed raiders. Nick, meanwhile, checked on JC's slight injury.

'We got six of them, Captain.' Gus made his report. 'Four of them are hell-bound and the other two are hit pretty hard . . . probably won't make it.'

'Several of the men who escaped were wounded,' Bob observed. 'The Maitland Guerrillas just got their tails kicked up between their shoulders.'

Nick thought about trying to grab up some of the horses and going after the remaining bandits, but JC was bleeding from his upper arm and one of the Simmons boys had a nasty crease along his neck that needed to be tended to. Plus, the two injured bandits would need a doctor's care if they were to survive.

'Tie the dead over their horses — if you can catch them. If not, we'll stick the bodies in the boot. Load the two wounded men into the coach and let's head for Denver.'

'Half of them got away,' JC griped, still sitting on the driver's box.

Nick sighed. 'If we'd had a few more

men, we would have had some following on horseback. We could have put an end to them once and for good.'

'Take the win,' Gus advised him. 'We made them pay dearly for this attempted hold-up.'

'One of the wounded is asking for the man in charge.' Andy spoke to Nick. 'He isn't going to make it back to Denver.'

Nick followed Andy over to a well-dressed bandit. He looked near forty years old, with gray above both ears, though his missing hat revealed he still had a full head of black, curly hair. His teeth were clenched against the pain of his bullet wounds, but he remained conscious.

'I'm Kilpatrick,' Nick said, kneeling down at the man's side. 'You said you wanted to talk to me?'

The man coughed and used one hand to cover two holes in his chest. 'Lex Bishop,' he gasped, trying hard to summon enough wind to speak. 'I used to be a gambler, but sold my soul to the

Devil.' He attempted a grin, but it was more a grimace. 'That would be Frank Maitland.'

'I believe he got away,' Nick told him. 'That's why I asked to talk to you.'

'I'm listening, Bishop. What can I do for you?'

'It's my wife,' he blurted, having to force out each word. 'She's with . . . ' He paused from a constriction that blocked his throat. A hoarse cough allowed him to get out a few more words. 'I'll tell you where to find Maitland, if you promise me you'll take care of my wife. She's innocent. Didn't know I was . . . ' He coughed again.

'All right,' Nick promised. 'I'll look after her. Just tell me where to find Maitland.'

Bishop could barely whisper; his lungs were filling with blood as the very life seeped out of his body. Nick put his ear close to the man's lips, trying to hear his mumbled whispers. When a sigh escaped the man's lips, Nick lifted his head and saw the glassy stare of

46

death and lax features of the man's face.

JC had wrapped a crude bandage about his upper arm as he walked over to Nick. 'What'd he have to say?'

'He didn't have enough time. I only have a vague idea of where he was talking about.'

'He give you the Maitland hideout?'

'Something like that.'

JC showed a skewed expression. 'Something?'

'Looks like the rangers have one more job,' Nick replied. 'Let's get these men back to town.'

'Yeah, but what's *something*?' JC continued to pester him.

Nick grinned. 'Don't worry, it's something you can probably handle by yourself.'

4

It was a dusty, dirty, bloody crew who showed up at the shack. Darlene had no experience with gunshot wounds, but she was escorted to the main house and drafted into service.

Skye had a nasty crease on his thigh and both Ken and Frank had several buckshot pellets in their upper body. Frank had only been hit with three tiny steel balls and they hadn't gone in very deep. Ken had taken a bit more of the blast, but the five pellets were all in or near his shoulder. Darlene used a pair of tweezers and a sharpened jackknife to get them out. Then the area was splashed over with whiskey to disinfect the area. The bandage was a piece of torn linen, to which Darlene added a thin layer of all-purpose salve that would protect the wound and keep the cloth from sticking while the punctures healed. Skye needed his wound cleaned and bandaged, but it stopped bleeding before they arrived. Once finished with the wounded men, Darlene paused to look out the window.

'Frank, you said Lex was bringing a couple of the extra horses. Where is he?'

'They suckered us in.' Frank swore bitterly, ignoring her question. 'I can't believe we didn't see it coming.'

'I was afraid we were tempting our fate by hitting the same stage for a third payroll,' Ken said. 'We were lucky to get away with our lives.'

'Killed half of our number,' Josh growled. 'They really suckered us in.'

'The one riding guard atop the stage was a holy terror with a gun,' Skye announced. 'Blasted Chavez and you two with the scattergun and then downed Toler with his handgun.'

'Looked like a green kid was driving the team.' Frank cursed more vehemently. 'Damn sneaky coyotes. His pretending to stop caught us napping.'

'Where is Lex?' Darlene shouted, unhappy at being ignored.

Frank shook his head. 'He was knocked from his horse by someone from inside the coach. I suspect he's dead or on his way to Denver by now.'

'What?' she cried. 'You told me he was a short way behind you.'

'I didn't want you getting all hysterical,' Frank replied. Shrugging off the lie, he added: 'Not until you got everyone bandaged.'

'But — ' she started to protest.

He threw her a hard look. 'We'll check out the news and see what happened to Lex in a few days. If he didn't buy the farm, we might figure a way to help him escape.'

'Do . . . do you know how bad he was hurt?' she wanted to know.

'I seen him go down,' Ken answered. 'Appeared he was hit a couple of times by the two shooters from the coach. There was too much lead flying around for us to stick around and examine his injuries.'

'So you deserted him? You left him behind?'

Frank stepped over and looked down at her. 'We would have left anyone who didn't stick in the saddle, woman. If it had been me or Ken — any of us — we'd have had to leave them behind. Lex was a good friend. I wouldn't have ridden away if there had been another choice.'

'What . . . what about me?' she asked. 'What am I supposed to do now?'

'You'll move out to the back porch for the time being. Once as we find Lex's fate, we'll decide what to do.' Frank's expression bore the edge of a man who would accept no argument or discussion. 'That's the end of it for now. You're going to do the cooking and cleaning to earn your keep. We have to wait and see what happens.'

Darlene lowered her head in a sign of obedience. She would wait until they learned of Lex's condition. After that she would make her own decision.

★ ★ ★

Sitting in a chair across from the mayor's desk, Nick was not satisfied with their results, but he was being told the job was over. The committee viewed the ambush as a total success, having driven off the Maitland Guerrillas and reduced their number by six men. As such, they didn't wish to fund the six rangers any longer. By inflicting such damage, the consensus was that it would deter the Maitland brothers from returning to Denver or the surrounding area.

'One of the dying gang members gave me a rough idea as to where the Maitlands' hideout is located. It's over in Wyoming so it might take a week or two, but I'm sure we can find it.'

'You said he wasn't specific, that he died before he could give you its actual location.'

'Yes, but he did say it was a short way from the regular stage route between Rio Blanco and Rimrock, near a trading post.'

'You are free to continue to hunt for the remainder of the gang, Kilpatrick. There is still a bounty of five hundred dollars for each Maitland brought in alive or dead.'

'Mayor,' Nick said, 'you know there are another dozen men who sometimes ride with the Maitland boys. They are bound to start robbing again.'

'Word will spread from the news account of your success,' the mayor assured Nick. 'We are hopeful some of the gang will split from the Maitlands. I mean, who is going to want to join a gang that suffered such a devastating slaughter as they did?'

'The bonus you promised wasn't as much as we expected.'

The mayor's face worked to mask his chagrin. 'I'm sorry about that, Kilpatrick, but the express companies and banks were counting on your rangers getting at least a couple of the Maitland boys. The others are small fish in comparison.'

'We were outnumbered two to one,'

Nick reminded him. 'If they had come at us with twenty men, we'd have all been killed.'

'I know it isn't what we hoped for, but it was still well worth your efforts. I mean, two hundred dollars each, above the salary we were paying — that's equivalent to several months' wages.'

Nick decided the matter was settled. When he didn't say anything more, the mayor asked about what the other rangers might do.

'The Simmons boys have a temporary job lined up here in Denver, while Gus and Loudermilk are going to work for a freighting outfit. JC is waiting to see what I'm going to do next.'

'And what are you going to do?' the mayor asked. 'Are you going to keep after the Maitland boys?'

'I promised a dying man I would find his wife and get her to safety. I mean to keep my word.'

'The reward for the Maitland boys is waiting,' the mayor reaffirmed. 'If you find them, bring them back . . . dead or alive.'

Nick rose to his feet and started to fork over the special 'Ranger' badge with which he and the others had been provided. The mayor lifted his hands, palms outward, to stop him.

'If you are going to keep after the Maitlands, you keep the badge. You are still empowered by the governor to act as a ranger.'

Nick laughed at the idea. 'I can't do much on my own.'

'If you find their hideout, you can recruit all the help you need to make the arrest. I realize it won't be easy, but I know you've got the smarts to get the job done. If anyone can track those polecats to their burrow, it's you.'

One of the businessmen added, 'With the reward money, you could start an outfit of your own — cattle, horses, a trading post or business of some kind. It's a big risk, but the reward is great.'

'Probably end up as a small headline for the local newspaper — Nicolas

Kilpatrick, another victim of the Maitland Guerrillas!'

'It always takes a measure of guts to attain the glory of victory,' the mayor stated with a grin.

Nick stepped away from his chair. 'I suppose I can give it a few weeks, at least until I run out of money.'

'You're a good man, Kilpatrick. I'll speak to the parson about offering a prayer on your behalf at the Sunday meeting.'

'Thanks, Mayor. I've a feeling I'll be needing the help.'

★ ★ ★

In the days that followed Lex's unknown fate Darlene continued to work long hours, cooking over a hot stove and taking care of four to six men. The daily toil grew worse as her tummy continued to expand. She would soon be a mother. On one particular night, as she was having a difficult time finding a position that would allow her to sleep, she overheard the Maitland men laughing and talking.

It was only the four brothers this night, drinking and playing cards, as they often did to pass the time. Darlene was careful to never be around when the men began to drink. After consuming a few shots of whiskey, they would often talk dirty and try to grab or pinch her if she got too close. She had learned to retire to the bedroom whenever the men got together for their fun and games.

This was one of those times when they had drunk more than usual and she could hear their boisterous partying. It was Dan's raucous laughter that got her attention.

'You're busted, Frank!' he whooped. 'Tens over sixes. I got you beat again.'

'By jingo! You've had the hot hand all night,' Frank complained. 'I never seen such a run of luck.'

'Want to go double or nothing?' Dan asked, his words slurred from too much drink.

'I've got nothing left to put up,' Frank replied, drink thick in his voice. 'I'm not gonna bet money we haven't stole yet.'

'Tell you what we should play for,' Josh spoke up in a semi-hushed voice. 'How about we put Darlene in the pot?'

Dan chortled with glee. 'I'd ante up for a chance at that.'

Darlene gasped in shock. Frank and Ken had been to the trading post that day. They must have learned of Lex's fate.

'You two are plumb loco!' Ken laughed, then proceeded to prove her fear correct. 'That gal ain't never gonna let either of you touch her.'

'Ken's right,' Frank joined in. 'Darlene swatted you a good one the last time you got too friendly with her, Josh.' He snorted with humor. 'Like to broke your nose!'

'That was different.' Josh sounded eager. 'Soon as we tell her that Lex ain't coming back, she is a widow without kith or kin.'

'So?' Dan asked.

'So we offer to make her a part of the family . . . for the sake of the child. Whoever wins the pot can marry her.'

'Whoa!' Dan sounded off. 'I ain't of a mind to get hitched to some woman and be forever stuck with her.'

'Plus there's the baby too,' Ken added. 'I don't see anyone at this table who's ready to be a father.'

Josh's voice again, both mocking and serious. 'I ain't saying one of us would marry her for real. It would all be make-believe.'

'Hey, that might work,' Dan voiced his support. 'You remember Hancock's hired hand? He once pretended to be a parson and faked a marriage for fifty dollars.'

'See?' Josh cried. 'We can play for Darlene and the winner will go along with the sham of getting hitched.'

Frank's voice came again, obviously speaking to Josh. 'I know you've had a flame burning for that gal since you first set eyes on her, but this? And you,

Dan, are you seriously thinking of playing cards to try and win a game where you pretend to marry a gal who's so pregnant she can hardly stand up?'

Josh guffawed. 'Geez, big brother, I ain't talking about any of us saying phoney vows to her right away. I'm talking about after the kid is born and maybe crawling or the like. You know, a few months down the road.'

'I don't know,' Frank said. 'Lex would come out of his grave spitting fire if he knew we had tricked his wife into a phoney marriage.'

'Lex was too durned old for Darlene,' Josh argued. 'He practically stole her from her cradle. And it ain't like I'm looking to get tied down for life.'

'So what? You keep her until you get tired of her,' Frank clarified. 'Is that the idea?'

Josh answered, 'Look at it this way, big brother. Darlene came into the gang when Lex joined us. We've supplied her room and board for months and she ain't got nowhere else to go. She owes us for all we've done for her.'

Dan jumped in again. 'You know, I think Josh has a good idea. Let's play a hand and see who gets to act the part of a new husband!'

'Not so fast,' Josh retorted. 'Anyone wanting in on this should fork over a sizeable ante.' A few seconds passed and he added: 'I'm tossing a hundred dollars in the pot. If any of you want to play for Darlene, you've got to match it.' He jeered, 'Besides, the winner is gonna' need to have a little extra money. It's expensive being a husband and a father!'

After some raucous laughter, Dan cried: 'Count me in! Here's my hundred.'

'I reckon I'm out,' Frank muttered. 'I don't have any money left other than our emergency stash. Besides which, I'm getting along in years. I don't want you boys calling me names behind my back like you did Lex.'

Ken chuckled. 'You just don't want to raise a second bawling brat — not after putting up with Josh all these years.'

There was another round of laughter.

'How about you, Ken?' Dan asked. 'Are you buying into this game?'

'I'm only two years younger than Frank, too blasted old to take on the chores of a family . . . even if it is a pretend marriage. I'll sit back and see which of you two younger bucks wins the pot.'

Darlene was crushed by the conversation. She sat in the dark aghast, suffering a terrible fear in her chest. She had found little to love about Lex. Once married to him, he showed his true nature, drifting from one town to the next, out all hours gambling. He enjoyed having someone handy to cook, do his laundry and keep his house, but he wasn't cut out to be a husband or father.

'One more thing, Josh.' Dan was speaking again. 'If I win, there's no saying how long I have to stay married to her.'

Josh laughed. 'That's easy enough to fix. If we can fake a marriage, we can also fake a divorce.'

'I don't know, boys,' Frank wavered. 'Maybe we ought to send her packing and get rid of them both. I mean, do we need a woman and kid in the house all the time?'

'You want to do the cooking, laundry and cutting of firewood?' Ken posed the question.

Frank again. 'Well, no, but I'm not real keen on the idea of having a snotty-nosed kid running around the house either.'

'If Darlene or the little imp becomes too much trouble, we can always give them the boot,' Ken replied to that.

'Then the game is between me and Dan,' Josh announced. 'If you want to change your mind, Dan, I'll lay claim to her here and now.'

'She don't even like you,' Dan shot back.

'What choice does she have?' Josh retorted. 'It's not like a lot of men want to take on an outlaw's widow and new baby.'

'OK, it's settled,' Frank declared. 'Let's see if it's going to be Dan or Josh who pretends to become Darlene's new husband.'

Darlene felt the sting of tears, but blinked them away. She had been sitting up in the dark, but the position was uncomfortable with the baby being more than eight months along. She lay back on her bed and stared up at the dark ceiling overhead. These past weeks, she had tolerated the crude and vulgar remarks and endless groping from the four Maitland men. But this? To be forced into a fake marriage?

She heard the laughter as the cards were being dealt. Once the baby was born, Frank and his brothers would give her the ultimatum. She was to marry whichever one won the card game. She wasn't a mother with child, she was the winner's pot. Only it would be a mock marriage. It was sick. It was indecent. It was sinful.

Married to a thief and murderer, all I have to offer a child is my personal honor. Now Frank and his brothers want to take that too!

5

JC had insisted on tagging along with Nick, but their initial search of the region had not turned up any information on the outlaw ranch Lex Bishop had described.

'We have to be within fifty miles of the place,' Nick told his young companion, as they took a break and let their horses drink at a stream. 'Lex said the ranch was across the Wyoming border, only a couple miles from a stage route and trading post. The problem is, he died before he could pinpoint the location, and the stage runs through a half dozen small towns between Laramie and Rio Blanco.'

'It's gonna take weeks of riding to check every trading post along the way,' JC said.

'It will be quicker if we split up,' Nick proposed. 'Each of us will follow the route in opposite directions. Be careful not to mention the Maitlands by name. We don't want to alert the gang that we're looking for them. Plus, they might have contacts or friends who would put a bullet in our backs.'

'I understand,' JC replied. 'We pretend to be looking for work or something and ask about any nearby ranches.'

'Yes. Once we find the place, we will contact the other rangers and get enough help to do the job right.'

'Shame to share the reward,' JC said, showing his cocky grin. 'The two of us could probably handle them, but I'd hate to see you get shot to pieces.'

Nick chuckled. 'Nice to know you are worried about my safety.'

'It's up to us younger guys to take care of you old-timers,' JC said with a grin.

Nick ignored the barb. 'You wire Rimrock in two days and Laramie in three. If I don't get the message at one place, I'll get it at the other. If I find something, I'll send a wire to you at Rio Blanco.'

JC parted with a wave and Nick turned in the opposite direction. The days of freedom for the Maitland gang were numbered. After they were taken care of, Nick would see about helping Bishop's wife get settled in Denver or Cheyenne. Lex claimed she was innocent of any wrongdoing. Therefore, she deserved a chance at a new life, away from outlaws and murderers. If it took a week or a month or even more . . . well, a promise was a promise; he would keep his word to the dying outlaw.

★ ★ ★

The following day, Nick arrived in Rimrock and checked the telegraph office. There was no word from JC. He hadn't really expected to hear from him yet, so he continued en route toward Laramie. He had gone a half-dozen miles when he topped a rise and paused to look down on the valley below. The main trail continued along the bottom of the hill and disappeared over the rise, probably a mile or so distant. Along the route, the trail dipped through several washes that emptied into a nearby stream.

Studying the terrain, he spotted a one-horse chaise, parked alongside the road. It struck him odd that such a buggy was this far from the nearest town. Even more curious was the fact that there didn't appear to be anyone around, not that he could see anyway.

Thinking the rig might be inoperative, or perhaps the horse had come up lame and the owner was afoot, he nudged his mare with his heels. The mount responded and proceeded at an easy canter down the slight rise, then broke into an easy lope to cover the remaining ground.

As Nick approached the buggy he spotted the outline of a body. There was someone lying on a blanket, a few feet off the trail. He blinked and squinted, attempting to focus his vision on something that seemed both bizarre and improbable. It looked like a woman was lying flat on her back, with her feet tucked tight against her thighs and her knees stuck up in the air.

Nick pulled his horse to a halting stop, jumped to the ground and hooked the reins over the railing on the carriage. Three steps took him to the lady and he suddenly grasped the situation. The woman was in hard labor.

OK, so Nick was a man with a bit of everyday knowledge. He knew that cows calved, horses foaled, dogs puppied and sheep lambed, but this? His singular experience with an actual woman giving birth was his own . . . and his memory of the event was less than distinct.

'Easy, ma'am.' He spoke gently to the lady. 'I seen your rig and thought you might be broke down.'

'Do I look broke down!' She hissed the words through clenched teeth, gasping and panting for breath.

Nick cast a yearning eye at his horse. He sorely wanted to jump in the saddle and skedaddle out of here. It would be a cowardly act, but the woman was in no condition to physically stop him. And who would ever know?

No! He shook the enticing thought from his head. To run from a woman in need would have haunted him for the rest of his life. Instead of swinging atop his mount and bolting for distant hill and prairie, he confusedly stared at the poor woman in wonder.

She was perspiring from the combined heat of the day and physical strain of childbirth. Beads of moisture dotted her brow and soaked her blouse. Her complexion was flushed and her damp, straw-colored hair was pasted to her scalp.

'D-don't just stand there,' she panted, her features drawn in agony. 'Do something!'

If ever a man wished he had taken a different trail — to be anywhere but here — it was Nick.

'What can I do?' he asked inanely.

'Of all the stupid . . . ' But her face flushed red, she again gnashed her teeth, then succumbed to a contraction and emitted an ear-piercing, agonizing wail. The woeful cry assaulted Nick's eardrums like the shriek of a banshee in a bear trap.

Forget pride, dignity and honor, Nick's brain demanded. *Get the hell away from this poor woman and save our sanity.*

But he endured the lady's terrible cry, until she recovered and finished. Then she threw her head from side to side, and gulped in several breaths of air. Nick steeled his resolve, mustered up his courage and dropped down on his knees at her feet. Lifting the woman's skirt, he summoned a respectful tone of voice and said: 'I sincerely beg your pardon, ma'am.' And he took a gander at the situation. The sight knocked him back on to his heels.

'For the love of . . . the baby's coming!' he yelped.

'Of course it's coming,' she fired back. 'Did you think I was having a picnic?'

'Well, can't you do something to stop it?' he entreated. 'I mean, you ought to try and wait a bit, until I can maybe find some help.'

She glared at him, an *are-you-really-that-dumb?* sort of look. However, when she spoke again, her voice was controlled.

'I . . . ' She set her teeth against the agony of another contraction and issued a plea. 'Please, mister. I-I can't do this by myself.'

Nick wished there was time to wash his hands, but the baby appeared fixed upon venturing forth to the outside world this very minute. Pushing up his sleeves, he clung to the single nerve holding his rationality together. There was no one else around. It was up to him. He glanced skyward and closed his eyes for a precious two seconds.

God, I reckon I ain't been the most saintly man, he prayed silently. *But please don't be looking the other way, 'cause I can really use Your help ... right now!*

★ ★ ★

It had been a five-day trip, over to the main roads and trails leading into and out of Cheyenne. The gang had hit two different stages and a trading post, wounding three people and killing one in the process. But, even robbing the passengers and customers too, they had come away with less than $600 for all of their work. They were not in a festive mood when they arrived back at their ranch. After five minutes, Frank was cursing and tearing the house apart.

'That dirty, ungrateful tramp!' he screamed. 'We gave her a home, with food to eat and a roof over her head. We took her in, as a part of our family, and she runs out on us.'

'Maybe she went for help to deliver the baby?' Josh ventured a thought.

'She might have walked to the

trading post.' Dan also made a suggestion.

Ken went to the cupboard, removed a jar from the top shelf and looked inside. 'I don't think so. The little thief stole our emergency stash of money.'

Frank snarled another oath. 'She done run off all right.'

'Who would have thought?' Dan said, totally awed. 'The gal was sticking out like a bloated calf when we left. She could hardly walk.'

'It's only a mile to Hancock's store,' Ken ventured. 'She could have made it that far on foot.'

Frank swore vehemently. 'There was over a hundred dollars in that jar. No telling where she went with that much money.'

'We can't let her get away,' Josh snarled. 'I won her fair and square. That haughty little tigress is going to serve me as my wife.'

'It was to be a pretend wedding,' Dan corrected. 'It ain't like you was really going to marry her.'

Josh swore at him. 'Just 'cause you lost your hundred bucks! You think this is funny.'

'No one thinks it's funny,' Frank said, getting between them. 'But we can replace the money. It might be best all around if we just forget about Darlene.'

'No way I'm doing that, Frank,' Josh declared.

'I suppose there's a chance she would turn us in for the reward money.' Ken tossed out the notion.

'It's possible,' Dan agreed. 'She didn't exactly have a lot of love for us.'

The oldest member of the family looked out the window. 'The sun is setting; it'll soon be dark. We aren't going to find anything stomping about in the black of night.'

'You guys do what you want,' Josh insisted. 'I've made up my mind. I'll have that gal for my own, come hellfire or forty days of rain.'

Frank knew Josh had lusted after Darlene from the day she and Lex had arrived. Now that the boy had a chance to have the woman as his own, nothing was going to stop him from trying. He didn't really think she would send the law after them, but who knew a woman's mind? Especially one with a new baby.

'She done us all dirt, stealing our money and running off like she done.' He made the decision for the four of them . . . as usual. 'And we can't be sure she will keep her big mouth shut. I reckon we best find that runaway and bring her back.'

'Probably the safest way to go,' Ken concurred. 'I'll tell Skye and Gato to gather fresh horses from the pasture for first thing in the morning. We can check at the trading post and see if Darlene caught the stage. Then we'll know which way she went.'

'She might have waved down the stage on the main trail,' Josh said. 'She would be aboard without us knowing.'

'If Hancock don't know anything, we'll split up in pairs,' Frank outlined. 'Two east and two west, with the other two going south. There isn't a decent trail going north for a hundred miles. Besides, she wouldn't head for the Dakotas; that's Indian country.'

'Plus, the main stage line runs east and west.' Ken agreed with the plan. 'If she went south, it would be by way of the way station at Antelope Ridge and she'd be headed for the railroad.'

'We could get the men from Shady Cove to lend a hand with the search,' Dan submitted.

'She's a lone woman about to have a baby,' Frank replied. 'We can handle this without involving the rest of the gang.'

'What if we drag her carcass back here and she don't care for the idea of marrying you, Josh?' Ken posed the query.

The youngest of the Maitland family replied in an icy tone of voice, 'If she refuses to go along, she can work and serve us all.' He snarled the next words: 'And she will do it while wearing chains around both ankles.'

Frank took charge of how to proceed. 'Let's get some supper started and turn in early. We'll hit the trail at first light and find the runaway cow before she can escape or spend all of our money.'

★   ★   ★

It wasn't the smoothest delivery, but Nick managed to coax the child into the world without losing his nerve or dislocating one of the poor little tyke's limbs. Once he'd cut and tied off the umbilical cord, he used his neckerchief to wipe the baby. Lastly, he wrapped the tiny little girl in the only clean thing he could find . . . his spare shirt.

The lady had recouped a measure of her strength and composure by the time he'd finished. She still lay on the blanket, perspiring, jaded and breathing heavily. However, when he brought the child to her, she eagerly accepted the tiny bundle.

'It's a girl,' he announced.

'Does she have all her toes and

fingers?' she enquired anxiously. 'Are her eyes crossed? Is there anything wrong with her?'

'She looks fine to me, ma'am,' he assured her. 'Cute as a pixie's ear.' Still standing over the infant and mother, he added, 'First time I ever held a newborn baby.'

'Really?' Her voice was laced with a teasing sarcasm. 'And you seemed so relaxed and confident . . . almost like an experienced midwife.'

Nick accepted the ribbing amiably. 'Well, to tell the truth, I've come across an orphaned baby or two while riding with the rangers, but I've never been involved in helping one to take her first breath.'

'You did just fine.' She praised his efforts.

He grinned and quickly fetched his canteen. Kneeling down at her side, he gave the lady a few sips of water. She was still ashen and exhausted, but managed a weak smile for his courtesy.

'I really have to thank you, mister,'

she said. 'I don't know how I would have gotten through the delivery on my own.'

'If you don't mind my asking, why are you so far from a town or help?'

'I was on my way to Lost Bow.'

'Is your husband there?' he asked. 'Maybe I could get word to him or — '

'My husband is dead.'

Nick felt an instant regret. 'I'm right sorry,' he sympathized. He frowned with confusion and commented, 'Your buggy is pointed west, while the junction to Lost Bow is east, back down this road a mile or two.'

'I know, but I was told this short cut would save me five miles.'

Nick scrutinized the meandering route up into the hills. 'I don't think you would have had a lot of luck taking a carriage up that way. It looks like a steep and narrow trail.'

'I discovered that about the time . . . ' she sighed. 'I was going to turn back for the junction, but then the baby decided she was ready to come. I had no choice but to try and deliver her here.'

'You shouldn't have been out riding alone, not in your condition.'

'I had no choice,' she retorted a bit curtly. 'And I thought I had more time. The buggy ride seems to have hurried things along.' She mellowed at once. 'It's . . . fortunate you came along. Where were you going?'

'I'm kind of drifting toward Laramie. My partner and I are trying to locate an outlaw band.'

'To join up?'

She appeared serious, so he smiled. 'No, ma'am. I'm a specially appointed ranger in service to the people of Colorado.'

'Colorado? But we're in Wyoming.'

'Yeah, but the men I'm looking for are wanted in several territories and states. I'll stay after them until I fulfill my assignment, even if I have to follow them into Mexico.'

The young mother didn't reply so Nick paused to glance at the sky. The sun was about to set. There wasn't time to take the woman to Lost Bow . . . or anywhere else. The closest bit of civilization was Rimrock, but even that was two hours away.

'It looks as if we're going to have to spend the night here,' he told the woman. 'I'll pull the buggy around and use the canvas I carry to make a lean-to.'

'I can't stay here,' the woman said quickly — a response that caused Nick to worry that something was amiss. Not that he was all that familiar with womenfolk, but the emotion in her voice was one of dread and concern.

'You're in no shape to travel, and your one-horse buggy doesn't allow you room to lie down. You need to rest up, at least for a day or two.'

'I'm sure I'll be all right,' she said defensively. 'You don't have to stay with me. I can take care of myself.'

Nick rubbed the three-day stubble on his chin. 'You talk like a hale and hearty woman, but when is the last time you gave birth to a baby?' He shook his head. 'If I was you, I wouldn't be too eager to bounce about on that buggy seat for a spell.'

His assertion stopped her cold. When she didn't offer to speak again he began the chore of erecting a shelter. He had a few supplies, enough to feed them both for a meal or two. When it came to the little sprout's care . . . well, he had helped bring her into the world, so now she was her mother's responsibility.

6

JC had entered the tavern and sat across from the old whip who drove the stage. After some small talk, he informed the driver that he was looking for his sister. He thought she lived along his route and she was married to a fancy-dressing gambler.

'Sounds like a little gal I've seen at Hancock's Trading Post on occasion. She was with some gent who looked like a dude.'

'That could be her. I think her husband was staying with some friends — Mainwaring, Marteen, Mattland . . . something like that.'

'Don't rightly know the names of any of the locals, but there are several farms and ranches near the trading post. She and the dude might be staying at one of them.'

'Well, say!' JC feigned happiness. 'It

sounds like Hancock is the man I need to talk to. I ain't seen my sister since she got married.'

'Hancock's place is down the road a fair piece . . . maybe six hours on a horse.' The driver grinned. 'I usually make it in five.'

'Yeah, I saw the draft team you're driving. They look like pullin' fools.'

'They've never let me down,' the driver bragged. 'That's one thing about this run, they provide me with good horseflesh. Back during the war we had mostly half-broke mustang stock and they weren't worth squat.' He chuckled. 'I'd wager most of them ended up on a spit over an Indian campfire, feeding a hungry tribe.'

JC laughed at his jest. 'Well, I drove a stage a few times out of Denver, but those animals would look downright pitiful alongside the team you're driving.'

'If I was heading west instead of east I'd let you tie your nag on back of the coach and you could spell me at the reins.' Another smirk. 'You'd get to see how a professional team handles.'

'Sure wish I was going the other way.' JC put a wistful look on his face. Then he smiled. 'But I ought to slip down and visit my sister. Maybe I'll catch up with you on your next run.'

The two of them shook hands and JC left the tavern. He had a solid lead, but what to do? Some of the trading posts had telegraph lines and some didn't. He decided he would have to take the chance and ride that way. He would send a wire to Rimrock, in case Nick hadn't gotten that far yet. Then he would do some snooping around and see if he could locate the Maitland hideout.

* * *

With the lean-to in place and the lady bedded down with her baby, Nick put her horse on a lead rope and rode his mount down to the creek for water. Luckily, he spooked a cottontail on the way back and shot it for supper. Once the horses were tethered for the night, he prepared the meat and used his frying pan to fix a meal of fried rabbit and spuds over a measured campfire. He also started a pot of coffee, placing it on a rock next to the flames, so it would begin to heat.

The woman dozed off each time the baby slept, but the smell of Nick's cooking brought her round. She seemed surprised to discover the moon was out, and silently watched him for a time without saying a word.

Nick fried the rabbit to a nice golden brown while he tended to the fried potatoes, keeping them separated. A tad of lard kept everything from sticking, but it still required his complete attention to not burn anything.

'I never asked you your name,' the lady said, breaking the long silence.

'Nick Kilpatrick,' he replied.

'My name is Darlene . . . ' She paused for a moment, then finished, ' . . . it's Darlene Bishop. As I said before, my husband died a few months back.'

Hearing the name Bishop, Nick just about dropped the skillet. It took a real effort to hide the immediate recognition. This was the woman he had promised to help. But how had she ended up so far from home? What about the new baby? And where was the gang?

'I'm right sorry for your loss,' he said, squashing the questions. 'It must be very hard on you, having to face giving birth and being on your own.'

'Yes. Yes, it is.'

Allowing that answer to suffice, he asked, 'How about the little tot? You give her a name yet?'

'I hadn't thought about it.'

He checked the meat a last time and found it was ready to serve. He first poured the lady a cup of coffee. Next, using his single tin plate, he dished up more than half the food for the new mother and set the frying pan aside. Providing her with his only fork meant he would eat with his knife and fingers.

He waited while Darlene laid the baby down, then passed her the plate and placed the cup at her side. He retrieved the frying pan and moved over to sit down next to her.

Darlene attacked the food with gusto. He wondered when she had eaten last. Of course, she had given birth too, so that probably added to her appetite. She also seemed to enjoy his coffee — something he would forgo until she finished. He could have drunk from the pot, but he didn't want the woman to think he didn't have proper manners.

Nick ate quietly, gratified that the rabbit had fried up perfectly. He allowed the woman to finish the meal without interruption. By the time she had sipped the last of the coffee, the baby was beginning to fuss.

'Sounds like someone else is ready for a meal,' he said, trying to act as if he was accustomed to such things.

'Yes,' Darlene replied uncertainly. 'I . . . I've never been around a baby before. I mean,' she hurried to correct the statement, 'I've seen a woman or two with her child, but I don't have any actual experience of being a mother.'

Nick chipped in a little of his own knowledge. 'Back on my folks' farm I helped to break a calf from nursing, but it's a mite early to stick your baby's nose in a bucket of milk so as to teach her to drink on her own.'

Darlene found his statement humorous and laughed. Nick smiled, feeling good to have broken the awkward tension.

'Good thing I'm not the one in charge here, huh?' he asked.

Darlene nodded her head, still amused. She said, 'I hate to have you do the cooking and also have to clean up after the meal too.'

'We've each got our chores cut out for us,' he replied. 'You tend to the baby and I'll take care of everything else.'

Darlene gave him an appreciative smile and began to prepare for the infant's first meal. Nick put his back to her and cleaned the pan and tin plate.

Afterwards, he had himself a cup of coffee . . . standing a few steps away, out in the dark. He knew some women were unflinching when it came to nursing — being it was a natural thing for mother and child — but he figured most would prefer not to have an audience. By his moving out of sight, it allowed Darlene a degree of privacy from a near complete stranger.

Nick aimlessly stared up at the stars. A half-moon glowed down from the heavens, a mystery about which he had often wondered. He knew nothing of astronomy or constellations, but he did recognize a few bright star groups that helped him to navigate when it was too dark for landmarks. A drover from Texas once told him that he and the other riders could tell time through watching the moon and the Big Dipper. The trick was that, as the moon passed from one particular star to the next, the night watch would know exactly when their relief was due to arrive. The herders didn't have to risk scaring the cattle by lighting a match to read a timepiece, because they could tell almost to the minute when the next shift was to start.

Staring at the heavens this night, Nick was struck by a new sensation — the wonder of life. He had no idea as to how God had created all things, but holding a new baby for the first time, it filled his mind and heart with awe.

'Mr Kilpatrick?' Darlene's voice broke his concentration.

He walked quickly back to the lean-to. 'I'm right here, ma'am.'

'I'm afraid Helen needs a change. She seems to have soaked your shirt.'

Nick stopped next to the fire. 'Helen? You've given her a name?'

'It was my grandmother's first name. I remember her from when I was a little girl. She used to tell me a story about a place called Troy, where a great war was started because of a beautiful woman named Helen.'

'Helen sounds like a good name,' Nick allowed. 'And she is definitely the most beautiful baby I ever saw.'

Darlene beamed at the compliment, then explained awkwardly: 'I didn't expect Helen to arrive so soon. I was going to sell the horse and buggy and buy the things I needed in Lost Bow.'

'You know someone there?'

'Not really,' she admitted. 'My husband told me he had a cousin, the man who runs a livery stable there . . . Cy Bishop. I've never met him.'

He didn't pursue the conversation and got back to Helen. 'You don't have anything we can use for the baby?'

'I left in a hurry and spent every last cent of my money to buy the horse and carriage.' The flickering firelight displayed her sheepish expression. 'I'm afraid I didn't even buy any food for the journey. If you hadn't come along . . . '

Nick didn't make her finish. 'I can take my spare shirt down to the creek and rinse it out, but we're going to need another cloth or two. Maybe you could take a piece of your petticoat and use that, just until we get to Lost Bow?'

'We?' She didn't mask her surprise. 'I thought you were on your way to Laramie.'

'I don't think I'll have to make that ride,' he said, knowing Darlene was the key to finding the Maitland gang.

Relief and gratitude infiltrated her expression. 'Oh, that would be a great help. I didn't know how I was going to drive the carriage and look after Helen too.'

'Like I said, it's no trouble.'

'Do you have a knife or something?' she asked, getting back to the present problem. 'We can cut my petticoat into four or five sections. Then we'll have plenty of changing cloths.'

Nick produced his skinning knife. Once Darlene had squirmed out of the garment, he followed her directions and began to slice it into pieces. When finished, they had four fairly clean cloths for diapers and two more that needed to be washed, along with his shirt.

Although it was dark he made the

trip down to the river and thoroughly rinsed out the items. Once back at camp he strung his rope between the wagon and the lean-to, making a clothes line. It meant rounding up some more wood for the fire, as he wanted everything to be dry by morning.

It was late when he eventually stretched out on his saddle blanket and leaned his weary head against his saddle. The lady had his bedding, but he used the rain slicker to cover himself and was able to doze off. Of course the little nipper, Helen, would likely wake up hungry every couple hours, so he wasn't going to get a lot of sleep anyway.

★ ★ ★

Frank led the way into Hancock's trading post. Dan, Josh and Ken were close on his heels, while Skye and Gato looked after the horses. One question was all it took to discover that Darlene had not stopped by or been seen.

They picked up a few supplies and then split up, with two men going in each direction. The idea was for each pair to contact the trading post and leave word. Once they discovered where Darlene was headed, they would all ride in that direction.

Ken and Skye rode south, although it was a long shot that Darlene would have gone that way. It was twenty-five miles of rough country to the railroad and there was little more than a small ranch or two along the route.

Josh and Gato took the trail west, riding hard and fast. They would proceed to Rimrock and see if the girl had been seen passing through town. It was a full day's ride on horseback, and Darlene was in no condition to make a ride at all. Still, she might have gone that way, thinking the opposite direction was the obvious route.

Frank and Dan took the most plausible choice, the road to Rio Blanco. It was less than ten miles, so it was the nearest place to buy a ticket on the stage, or maybe hitch a ride to Cheyenne. A pregnant woman, especially one who looked about five minutes away from giving birth, would not be hard to follow.

7

Nick used a good portion of his remaining supplies to prepare breakfast for himself and Darlene. She had good color, but he didn't figure she was ready to sit astraddle of a bucking bronc just yet. Not that she complained, but Nick noticed how every movement caused her a measure of discomfort.

'I'm going to take the horses down to the creek for water,' he announced, once he'd finished eating. 'I'll stake them where there is plenty of grass and then see if I can catch us some fish for supper.' He waited to allow her to comment. When she offered nothing, he continued: 'I think you had better rest up today. I've got enough food to get us through and I can wash Helen's diapers down at the stream as the need arises.'

'Why are you taking such good care

of me?' Darlene asked. 'You've already done much more than common courtesy demands.'

'I believe it's a man's duty to look after them that need it, Mrs Bishop.'

A smile surfaced on her lips. 'You are not at all like the other men I've been around, Mr Kilpatrick. You are caring and considerate.'

'My mother once told me the world wouldn't be worth shucks if men stopped behaving like gentlemen and women quit being ladies.'

'You don't know if I'm a lady or not,' she replied. 'As for bringing Helen into the world, any female of the proper age can have a child.'

'I reckon you're right, ma'am.'

'Do you have a wife or special girl?'

'Never found the time. I spent the last few years chasing after Indians or bandits. It didn't leave a lot of time for chasing girls.'

'And now?'

'Once I finish this job, I should have enough money to start something of my own . . . maybe a small business or ranch.'

Darlene grew serious. 'It could be dangerous for you to stay here with me.'

'Why do you say that?'

'I . . . it isn't safe,' she stammered. 'There might be some men looking for me.'

'Might be?'

'It's not that I'm all that important to anyone, but I took some grocery money when I left the place I was staying. And the men my husband worked with — one of them thinks I belong to him.'

'Why would he think that?'

Darlene delayed the answer, as if thinking it over. 'It's hard to explain,' she admitted at last.

Nick didn't let the matter drop. 'You said your husband died. Why would some other man think you belong to him?'

Darlene hesitated, seemed to do a little soul-searching, then blurted out her life's story.

She told him how her father died in a

mining accident when she was eleven. She was an only child, so her mother took her and moved to Denver, Colorado, to live with her spinster sister. Two years later, her mother came down with pneumonia and died after a few weeks, leaving her in the care of her aunt.

'Lulu was not a happy woman,' she expounded. 'She ran a laundry and I became her personal slave. Sixteen-hour days of washing and ironing at the laundry, plus I was also expected to help cook and clean around the house. Lulu called it home, but my room was a tiny attic above the laundry. For six long years, I worked at the endless tasks, wearing throw-away clothing that was left at the laundry and suffering as part of Lulu's unhappy existence. Then Lex Bishop came through the door.'

Darlene admitted how she had been beguiled by his smooth talking and his fancy clothes. He told her she was pretty and swept her off her feet. The man was twice her age and quit his job to join an outlaw gang. She proceeded to tell Nick of overhearing the card game and how she was going to be expected to accept a phoney marriage with one of the bandits. She finished with, 'I couldn't live under those circumstances, so I ran away.'

She fell to silence, so Nick brought her back to their present situation. 'How about this man, your husband's cousin, the one you are going to try and find at Lost Bow?'

'I'm not sure he is still living there . . . or if he's even alive, for that matter.'

'If he is there, what kind of help can he be?'

'I'm hopeful he will let me stay with him a little while, until I can find a way to take care of Helen and myself.' She uttered a worried sigh. 'However, I'm going to show up on his doorstep without having ever seen him. I'm not sure of the reception I'll get.'

'Come tomorrow or the next day, when you're up to the trip, we'll ride to

Lost Bow and find out.'

She didn't speak the next question — *what to do if Cy was no longer alive, or if he had left the country.* Instead, she again rewarded him with a timid smile and said, 'I'm beholden to you, Mr Kilpatrick.'

Nick hesitated. He should tell her about his involvement in her husband's death. She had a right to know. She had been truthful with him; he should be truthful with her. Before he could confess, Helen began to fuss and the moment was lost.

Nick cleaned and put away the few items of dish-ware, then collected a couple of the improvised diapers that needed washing. He next picked up the two horses, but, as it wasn't a long walk to the creek, he didn't saddle his mount. He did take time to round up his hook and fishing line.

The sun was up and warming the day. He would tether the horses where they could get some good feed, then wash out the garments and hang them over brush to dry. After that, he would cut himself a short pole, hunt up some grubs for bait and try his luck along the stream. If he didn't catch a couple fish, he would have to hope he could scare up another rabbit or sage hen. This business of being the provider for a family was a real chore, but it did add to man's feeling of self-worth.

* * *

Frank Maitland paced back and forth while the horses drank their fill. They had reached Rio Blanco and found the man who had sold a horse and buggy to Darlene. The fellow couldn't be sure, but he thought she went back toward Rimrock.

'It makes no sense,' Frank told Dan. 'Why come this far east and then turn around and head west? Unless she only meant to throw off any pursuit.'

Dan had been considering the news as well. 'I think I've got it figured out.'

At Frank's inquisitive frown, he continued: 'I'll bet the stage picked her up on the road.'

'Of course it did,' Frank growled impatiently. 'She couldn't have walked this far.'

'No, listen to me.' Dan explained, 'It didn't matter which way the stage was going . . . either here to Rio Blanco, or the other direction to Rimrock. Darlene would have been desperate for transportation; she was afoot. The stage came along and she hopped on. Then she gets off here in Rio Blanco and uses the money she stole to buy a horse and buggy. Once she has her own transportation, she goes the direction she intended all along.'

'I get what you're saying,' Frank said. 'She would have taken the stage to Timbuktu, if it was passing by, just so she could get to a place where she could buy a rig of her own.'

'And she wanted to go west.' Dan continued with the notion. 'If she was going to Denver or Cheyenne, she could have bought a ticket on the stage. She spent most or all of her money on the carriage, meaning she must have had a place in mind from the start.'

Frank rubbed the scruffy beard that covered his chin and declared, 'You're right, little brother. She was only after her own transportation.'

'That's the way I figure it, Frank.'

Frank's brain sifted through everything he could remember from when Lex had talked about his wife's family. Darlene had been living with an aunt and was pretty much alone in the world. She had married Lex to escape working in a laundry and often swore she would never go back there. As for Lex, he had mentioned a cousin or something one time. Everyone else he knew had lived back on the east coast. Frank racked his brain, seeking the lost tidbit of information in his mind. It was no use. It had been too long ago and it was an off-hand comment. He had been busy planning a job or drinking at the time. He had barely heard the words.

He told Dan about the conversation and finished with, 'I'll bet you a gold eagle she is trying to reach Lex's kin.'

Dan was confused. 'I never heard Lex talk about any kin.'

'He only mentioned it the one time — an uncle or cousin, I think. He must have told Darlene about him and he's the man Darlene is looking for.'

Dan's voice was cynical. 'That's not much help. We still don't have any idea where she is going.'

'No, but we know it's close enough for her to think that she could reach it by carriage. If the guy was in another state or territory she would have taken the stage or train.'

'She would have done the same if she returned to the laundry in Denver. That means we're looking for a smaller town, one not along the tracks, and the stage was going the wrong way.' Dan rubbed his hands together while voicing his logic. 'It can't be too far away. In her condition, she would be crazy to travel any real distance.'

'First thing, we need to make certain she didn't continue east. We'll go as far as the next place to get food or water. If no one has seen her, we'll head back to the trading post and see if there's word from Josh or Ken.'

'Good thinking, Frank. We don't want to let her trick us into going the wrong way.'

'If the little beggar doesn't run into a lawman, we'll catch her.' Frank pounded a fist into the palm of his other hand. 'Yes siree, she won't cross us again, not as long as she lives.'

★ ★ ★

Josh and Gato asked around at the town of Rimrock and found a storekeeper who had seen a lone woman come through town driving a buggy. They described her and he agreed it must have been Darlene.

'Funny thing,' the man said. 'The lady stopped at the watering trough and let her horse drink. Meanwhile, she climbed down from the carriage and came up to the water pump. She moved like she was heavy with child, though she wore loose clothing so it was hard to tell from a distance.

'The reason I remember her is that she worked the pump handle and drank right from the spigot. Most womenfolk would have stepped inside the café or asked at the store for the loan of a tin cup, but she used her cupped hands instead.'

'Is that all?' Josh asked.

'I heard her ask a guy on the street for directions to Lost Bow.'

Josh thanked the man and sent a wire to Hancock's trading post. He left word for his brothers that they were on Darlene's trail. Then they put their horses up at the livery where they could get plenty of food and water. Regardless of his desire to catch up with the woman, Josh knew their horses were beat.

'We'll have something to eat and

maybe try and catch a couple hours of sleep. The horses should be ready to go in four or five hours.'

'Darlene will have reached Lost Bow by now, unless she had the baby along the trail,' Gato told him. 'Maybe we should wait for Frank and the others?'

'That would take a couple of days. We can't let her get too well hidden. No telling what she has in mind.'

'You got any idea why she headed for Lost Bow?'

'Got me stumped. I never heard Darlene or Lex speak of knowing anyone over this way. But I never talked much to Lex about his pals or kinfolk.'

'Yes, all I ever heard him talk about was gambling.'

'You know anything about Lost Bow?' Josh asked.

'I went through there a few years back. It's not much of a town. I would guess there's no more than fifty people living in or around there. The main trail runs from here to Laramie. Those going through Lost Bow are mostly travelers and pilgrims from the Oregon Trail. It used to be a wild town, back when Fort Caspar was in operation, but after the army abandoned the fort, it about died out. A few of the original business owners are still around and there is a handful of farmers and ranchers up that way.'

'No sheriff or lawman in town?'

'Not enough people or money for that. I think the store and the saloon are the two major buildings, and there was a livery-blacksmith operation at one end of town. That's about all I remember.'

'Won't be any place for her to hide if she's there.'

'I know of a cut-off that runs through the hills.' Gato remembered the terrain. 'I recollect it saves several miles over taking the main road. It's too rough for a wagon, but no problem for a horse.'

'Good thinking,' Josh told him. 'We'll take the short cut and make up some time. Even with a carriage, I can't imagine Darlene going very fast over these roads.'

'She looked ready to pop before we left her at the ranch. Hard to believe she decided to run off. I mean, with a baby on the way and being safe at the ranch, why would she do that?'

Josh led the way to a café and they sat down to order a meal. Every desire in his body was to trade horses and ride, catch up with Darlene before she could get any further away. But he had to be patient. He had wanted Darlene since he first laid eyes on her, but Lex was handy with a gun. As long as he had been alive, Darlene had been out of reach. Now, after getting his brothers to agree, and winning the poker hand — she was his!

'You know,' he spoke up, reminded of the poker game. 'I'll bet Darlene overheard us playing cards, the game we had just before we left for our last raid.'

'Why would a card game be important?'

'It was just the four of us,' Josh explained. 'You and Skye were out in the bunkhouse.' Then he related to Gato about the wager and how they had agreed that he and Dan would play a game to see who was going to pretend to marry Darlene. When he finished, he bobbed his head. 'Yep, that's what happened. Darlene was eavesdropping and got her dander up. She always treated us Maitlands like we had a sack of smallpox tied around our necks. Never said a decent word to any of us.'

'Skye and me would agree with that. She acted mighty uppity for a gal whose husband was old enough to be her father and was nothing but a robber and thief.'

The two of them paused long enough to order a meal. Then Josh leaned over the table and said, 'We get that gal back and things will change. Once she thinks the two of us are married, she'll learn a whole new set of rules.'

'If she did overhear you guys, she might have heard the part about the marriage being fake too.'

'Maybe,' Josh admitted. 'If she did, I'll find some other way to make her behave. I'm not going to get tied down for the rest of my life, but ... ' he vowed, his jaw set and eyes glowing with frost, 'I'm going to have that woman as my own, no matter what!'

8

Nick washed and shaved at the creek, then caught five native trout in the next two hours of fishing. They weren't much for size, eight to ten inches in length, but they would suffice for supper. He also found some wild currant bushes and was able to collect a fair-sized handful. He checked on the horses about noon, moving them to allow them to both graze and reach the water. Lastly, he filled his canteen from a small trickle of water from an underground brook. It fed into the main creek and the water was pure and fresh.

When he got back to camp Darlene was on her feet. She smiled, seeing he had brought a string of fish.

'You're a good provider, Mr Kilpatrick.'

'Are you sure you should be up and

around?' he asked.

'I need to visit the stream to wash . . . both myself and my clothes. I think I'm up to making that much of a trip and back.'

'If you wash your clothes, what are you going to wear?'

'I'll use the blanket until everything dries enough to put back on,' she explained. 'I need to do it during the heat of day.'

'And the baby?'

'Helen has a full tummy and is asleep. She shouldn't get hungry before I get back.'

'You trust me with your little girl?'

The familiar smile curled at the corners of her mouth. 'Yes, Mr Kilpatrick, I trust you to watch over Helen.'

Nick went over to his saddle-bags. He hooked the fish on the carriage wheel, set down the canteen and put away his razor. He kept out his wash cloth and bar of soap. 'I don't carry a regular towel for drying,' he informed her. 'But you're welcome to use these.' And he handed them over to Darlene.

'I'll be back as soon as I can,' she said, thanking him with a bit wider smile. 'You and Helen stay out of trouble.'

He watched her walk gingerly along the trail he had followed to the water's edge. Checking to see that Helen was sleeping peacefully, he decided that when Darlene returned he would hunt up some more wood for the fire. He only had one potato left, but it, the fish, wild currants and a tin of beans would be enough to get them by. Come tomorrow, Darlene ought to be ready to travel.

Thinking of the new little mother, this delay had put him off schedule. If they had a telegraph office in Lost Bow he would leave word for JC at Rio Blanco. He was pondering over whether he should tell Darlene about his part in Lex's death when Helen began to fuss. He carefully picked her up using both hands, tucked her into the crook of his arm and spoke soothingly to her. She quieted down at once, as if mesmerized by the sound of his voice. The tiny tot's eyes were open and she seemed quite content to be held in his arms.

Nick felt a lump form in his throat, completely awestruck by the extraordinary sensation of holding a baby. Absently, he compared the attraction he felt for Helen to the intriguing mystery of looking into Darlene's bright, dark-chocolate-colored eyes. To this point in time, Darlene's hair had been mussed and unkempt, but he deduced it was as fine as blond threads of corn-silk. When loose and dangling about her face, he imagined it would decorate her features like an attractive silk scarf. Petite in build, she still had womanly proportions, a smile that made his knees weak, and when she had laughed, it resonated as music from a heavenly choir.

Nick continued to study the wondrous creation of life in the crook of his arm. He smiled as the baby's lips puckered and then meshed, doing a bit of imaginary suckling. Within her delicate features he could see the resemblance between mother and daughter. Both of them were precious, delightful and beautiful.

He chuckled at the ridiculous notion of having such feelings about a bandit's wayward widow and her new baby. He had obviously been seduced by the arrival of Helen and it was impossible to yet know Darlene's overall character. Additionally, the woman had been living with a bunch of outlaws, and he had helped to kill her husband. Allowing his mind to wander off on a romantic journey concerning the new widow was like running along the rim of a deep canyon while blindfolded.

* * *

Gato had reservations about going after Darlene without Frank giving the order. He would have preferred to wait in Rimrock until the others arrived. But Josh had his mind made up. If they allowed Darlene too much lead time, she could possibly end up hidden away where it would take weeks to find her. Two more possibilities — she might find a lawman and seek protection, or a compassionate family might take her in and put up a fight on her behalf. He decided Josh's way made sense. Find the girl before she had time to get help, and then head back to Rimrock. By the time Frank arrived, Darlene would already be under their control.

It was late afternoon when they reached the junction to Lost Bow. Gato said it was another mile or so to the short cut, so they rode past the main turn-off and continued along the river trail. They had traveled about ten minutes when Gato spied the buggy, sitting on the side of the road.

'There!' he said, pointing down the trail. 'That has to be the carriage Darlene bought. It's a one-horse shay, the small kind with a single seat.'

Josh had spotted it too. 'Yeah, cheapest buggy on the market — fits what she could afford with the money she stole. It looks like she threw up some kind of lean-to.'

'There's someone moving,' Gato said. 'Looks like Darlene. See? Right next to the carriage.'

'Yeah, but where's the horse?'

'Could have gotten loose and run off.'

'Be just like the little chowder-head,' Josh sneered. 'If she's afoot, we'll have to use one of our animals to pull the buggy.'

'She probably has him tied off in the brush where he can graze.'

'You take a look around for the horse, Gato. I'll take charge of our fugitive.'

They started forward together, until Gato turned off at a gully and began making a circle through the brush and choppy terrain to see if he could locate Darlene's horse.

Josh didn't get far before Darlene saw him coming. She grabbed up a bundle — it looked like a baby — and swung about as if searching for an escape. Josh kicked his mount into a lope and bore down on her. He felt an instant satisfaction as she discarded the idea of trying to run.

'That's right, you runaway mustang,' Josh goaded her, slowing to a walk and drawing closer. 'We've come to take you home . . . back where you belong.'

Darlene's expression was one of defeat and Josh observed that she looked surprisingly clean. Her hair was loose about her shoulders and the breeze blew a few strands into her face. She held a mostly covered infant tightly to her breasts. However, when she spoke, there was defiance in her heated words. 'I don't *belong* to you or anyone else, Josh. Lex is dead. I have my own life to live.'

Josh pulled his steed to a stop a few feet away and stared down at her with a satisfied smirk. 'You've got it turned backwards, Darlene honey. You belong to all of us; you're part of our family.'

'I'm not going to be your personal

slave,' she vowed vehemently. 'I only want to be left alone.'

Josh dismissed her anger. 'We'll discuss it when we get home. Where did you leave your horse?'

Darlene took a fleeting glance toward the stream and shifted her stance nervously. It could have been anxiety over being caught, but it seemed more than that.

Josh took a gaze in that direction and smiled. 'Oh, so you picketed the horse down by the creek.' He uttered a smug chortle. 'Well, don't you worry none, Gato is making a sweep of the area. He'll find him quick enough.'

'You and your brothers don't need me,' she protested. 'I've got a baby to tend and care for. I won't have time to do all of the chores and cooking for you and the others.' In a cold, warning tone, she added: 'And, no matter what you do or say, I will never let any of you touch me!'

'Don't know why you want to make this so hard, Dar'ling.' He purposely slurred the word to mimic her name. 'Me and my brothers settled everything; you're going to marry me.'

'I know the truth about that.' Her temper flared. 'The marriage is a trick, a despicable lie. I heard you talking about it.'

Rather than deny it, Josh grinned. 'No one is going to know the difference, Dar'ling. Besides,' he snickered, 'I'll build a new cabin, so we'll have our privacy and you can tend to just me and the kid. What more could you want?'

'I want a life of my own, a decent life for my daughter . . . away from a gang of murdering bandits. I'm not going with you, so go away and leave me alone.'

Josh glowered down at her. 'You'll soon learn to harness that tongue of yours, woman. I'm taking you back with me whether you like it or not.'

'I have to argue that point with you, mister,' a cool voice came from behind Josh.

He whirled in the saddle to see a man standing behind him. The guy had been carrying an armload of branches and wood for the fire, but dropped them in a pile at his feet. He appeared to be in his mid- to late twenties, capable-looking, with a ready gun on his hip.

'Who are you, and where the devil did you come from, fella?' Josh demanded to know.

'Name's Kilpatrick. And the lady has told me that you have no legal right to take her and her baby anywhere. The little bit of money she took doesn't begin to cover the months she worked and slaved for your family.'

'She's a thief!' Josh barked forcefully. 'And she belongs to me!'

'The lady says differently.'

Josh sneered, 'Well, the wick on her candle don't burn all that bright, bucko. She sometimes don't know her own mind. Trust me when I tell you, her future is with me.'

'If you are one of the Maitland pack, I don't see you having much of a future,' Nick said with finality. 'Now, I'd be obliged if you would leave, peaceable like.'

Josh turned his horse so that he had a clear line of sight at the man. His blood boiled in his veins and his eyes glowed hot with insolence. 'You'd be *obliged*, would you?' he taunted Nick. 'Well, I'd be *obliged* if you minded your own damn business.'

'I'm making the lady and her baby my business,' Nick replied. 'Ride away and don't look back.'

Josh rested his hand on his gun. He had a good mind to put an end to this buttinski! If Gato wasn't off looking for some blasted horse this guy wouldn't talk so tough. Even without Gato, it was real tempting to . . .

'Don't do something you won't live to regret,' Nick warned, evidently reading his thoughts.

Oh, yeah? This joker is asking for it. Well, Josh had seen his kind before, playing the bold hero, acting big for some strumpet. He would call this drifter's bluff and put a hole through his chest!

Josh jerked his gun free from its holster, thumb cocking back the hammer, finger finding the trigger smoothly as he brought the weapon up to fire. Frank and his other brothers were going to be in for a shock when they arrived. Not only had he gotten the girl back, he had killed —

Something slammed into Josh's chest with the force of a sixteen-pound hammer. The pistol flew from his fingertips, his horse jumped from the sound of a sudden gunshot, and Josh reeled from the saddle. The impact as he hit the earth didn't faze him, even though his head and body bounced off of the ground from the hard contact.

There was no sound, no smell, and nothing felt real. Josh opened his eyes to stare at the morning sky. Everything looked dim and out of focus. Then a cloud of darkness swept over his vision and all sensation was lost. His last glimmer of realization was of an infant near by, screaming loudly.

'Look out!' Darlene cried a warning to Nick.

A Mexican rider appeared, not more than thirty steps away. He had his gun out and threw a hasty shot in Nick's direction, but the bullet sailed harmlessly over Nick's head. Before Nick could return fire, the man yanked his horse around and dug in his heels. Ducking low over the saddle, he streaked through the brush and raced down the trail. Nick didn't have a clear shot and, within seconds, the rider was a quarter-mile away and still going at a full gallop.

Nick quickly looked around, wary, in case any more riders were near by. After a visual sweep of the area, he decided there had only been two men.

'The one on the ground is Josh Maitland,' Darlene told him, her voice quivering over the frightened crying of her baby. 'The man who rode away is Gato. He works with Frank and the others.'

Nick checked on Josh, but his body was already growing cold to the touch. He slowly approached the man's horse, which had shied away from the gunfire. After coaxing the animal into allowing him to catch up the reins, he loaded Josh's body over its back.

'If they have a telegraph at Lost Bow,' he said to Darlene when he'd finished, 'I'll wire the US marshal's office and report the shooting.'

'You might have been killed,' Darlene murmured, having hushed Helen by cuddling her close. Moving over to where she could look Nick in the face, she asked, 'Why did you risk your life for me?'

'Man does what's right or he ain't much of a man,' Nick replied.

Darlene had a perplexed look on her face. 'You sure don't fit into the same category of men I've lived around since I left my aunt's care.'

'Is that a good thing or a bad thing?' Nick asked.

A softness entered her features and

there was a slight upturn at the corners of her mouth. 'Oh, it's a good thing. It's just something I've never seen much of.'

Nick realized he was gawking at the young lady like a teenage boy who had just seen his first pretty girl. The warmth in Darlene's voice caused a constriction in his throat. He swallowed self-consciously and got back to their present situation.

'There's something I ought to tell you, ma'am,' he managed weakly. 'I put it off until . . .' He lowered his head, unable to meet the warmth and appreciation within her gaze.

'Yes?' she coaxed, as he struggled for the words that would make him out to be as deceitful as he was feeling.

'I told you I was searching for a gang of bandits.' Nick finally got his voice working again. 'Well, it's the Maitland gang I'm after.'

Darlene gasped. 'You're after the Maitlands?'

Nick explained about the hold-up

attempt and how he and his five rangers had downed half of their number. Then he explained about Lex and his final words. He finished with, 'So, even though Bishop was a bandit, a member of a gang that has killed no fewer than a dozen people over the last few years, his last wish was that I find you and help you start a new life away from the Maitland boys.'

'Why would he ask you to do that?' she queried. 'I mean, why you personally?'

Nick found the courage to look the woman in the eye. 'I was the one who devised the ambush, the one in command. Those other men were working under my orders.'

The woman's eyes narrowed with suspicion. 'Were you the one who shot my husband? Is that why you came looking for me?'

Nick sighed. 'No, Lex was shot by my men in the coach, but it was my plan. I'm the one responsible for his death.'

Darlene lowered her eyes and remained

in a personal reverie for a short time. Nick didn't speak again, allowing her to process the information. After a bit the lady's gaze lifted to meet his own.

'What do you intend to do about me?'

'I'm going to keep my promise to your husband,' Nick informed her. 'He said you were innocent and didn't know about the Maitland gang until after he joined up with them.'

'No, I didn't,' Darlene said.

'Then I'll find you someplace safe, a place where you can start a new life.'

Darlene firmed her features, having made a decision. 'There are over a dozen men who sometimes ride with Frank Maitland. They all rode with him during the war. You can't expect to protect me from fifteen or twenty men.'

Nick released the breath he had been holding, relieved that Darlene did not blame him personally for the death of Lex Bishop. However, the tenderness had left her voice and the eyes were aloof and lacked the warmth he had seen earlier.

'I can get more help,' he replied. 'Once we arrest Frank and the others, you will be safe and can start over.'

Darlene sighed. 'Well, I guess you won't need me to lead you to the Maitland hideout. Frank dearly loved Josh. When he learns that you killed him he will gather his men and follow us to the ends of the earth.'

Nick dismissed her warning as unnecessary. 'I'll harness your horse and tie my and Josh's mounts to the back of the shay. Then we'll go back to the fork and ride until it gets dark. We can make camp away from the trail and get an early start for Lost Bow in the morning. No telling how long we'll have before Gato makes contact with more of the Maitland bunch.'

'Whatever you say, Mr Kilpatrick,' Darlene said without emotion. 'It would seem my life is in your hands.'

9

Frank had been pacing for two hours before Ken and Skye arrived. After reaching the railroad they had sent a wire back to Hancock's and learned of Josh being on Darlene's trail. Their horses were lathered from the hard ride back to the ranch and both men looked as if they hadn't slept in two days.

'We came as fast as we could,' Ken told Frank. 'Like to have kilt off our horses getting back here.'

'Things have gotten a whole lot worse,' were Frank's first words to Ken. 'Hancock sent his errand boy with a second wire from Gato. He's in Rimrock, but Josh has been killed.'

Ken was stricken with an immediate grief. 'No!' he cried. 'How did that happen? I thought he had found Darlene's trail and was waiting for us to join him.'

'Gato telegraphed to say Josh wanted to catch Darlene before she got any farther away. Problem is, Darlene has joined up with some gunman. Josh tried to shoot it out with him and lost the fight. Gato said he got there after the shooting and rode back to Rimrock to send us word.'

'Why didn't Josh do like he was told?' Ken lamented. 'The knothead never listened to orders worth a damn.'

'We have fresh horses in the corral and picked up some supplies from Hancock's place.'

Skye asked, 'Do we know where Darlene was going?'

'Gato thinks she is headed for Lost Bow. It's the only town this side of Laramie that isn't near the railroad. There's no law in a town that small, but it must be where Lex's relative hangs his hat. It's the only thing that makes sense,' Frank explained.

'I can't believe it,' Ken said sadly. 'Josh is dead.'

Dan snorted his contempt. 'Getting

that blasted woman back wasn't worth Josh getting killed.' He swore savagely. 'Why did she have to run off!'

Frank's shoulders sagged with guilt and grief. 'I'm betting she heard us playing cards the night before we left to pull those jobs near Denver. Being in a family way, she got herself a bad case of pious and proper.'

'Who would have thunk?' Ken spoke again. 'I guess we should have left things like they were. She was a fair cook and housekeeper.'

'We shouldn't have made so much noise,' Dan spoke up. 'Having her hear us playing cards for her like we would for a horse was the mistake.'

Frank gave a negative shake of his head. 'The blame is mine for keeping her around without ever setting down any rules. She was either one of us, willing to accept the life we offered, or she was out on her bucket!'

'She would have probably left and starved to death on her own,' Dan surmised. 'You know how headstrong she was about being a proper wife. Remember how she hit Josh when he tried to get a little kiss?'

'Lex wasn't dead when she done that,' Ken interjected.

'Well, no, but anyone could see that Darlene never liked Josh.'

Frank waved a hand to dismiss the chatter. 'Trade out your horses,' he told Ken and Skye. 'If that gal has herself a gunman, we'd best round up the rest of the boys.'

'Some of them are a mite skittish since the ambush,' Dan warned.

'They either ride with us on this job or they can starve.' Frank snarled the words. 'We've been keeping twenty men fat and sassy with our hold-ups. Only the six of us went on every job, while they got to pick and choose. Well, this is not one of those times. I want every man jack who has ever rode with us . . . and I want them saddled and ready to ride by tomorrow.'

'I'll round up the men from Shady Cove,' Skye promised. 'They might leave a man or two behind to watch over their cattle and such, but I'll bring the rest of them.'

'It's a full day's ride to Rimrock. We won't catch them tomorrow.'

'Get things organized and then we'll grab a night's sleep,' Frank instructed.

There was logic in his order, but Frank didn't want to wait. Some drifter with a gun had killed their little brother. And the widow they had taken in and cared for had stolen their money and run off. Now she was responsible for Josh being dead. The desire for vengeance was great.

Dan patted Frank on the shoulder. 'We'll have everything ready by daylight, big brother. Gato will be waiting for us when we arrive at Rimrock.'

He waited, but Frank did not reply, consumed by a bitter mixture of sorrow and rage. He was the eldest, the one the others looked up to. He had to think of everyone else, not just himself. Allowing Josh to go with Gato had been a mistake, because Gato had let Josh take charge. He should have kept Josh with him and split it up so Dan or Ken would have been the ones to find the girl's trail. Either of them would have been smart enough to wait for the others. Josh was too eager to prove himself a man . . . and it had cost him his life. He bobbed his head after a moment or two in a sign of agreement.

'Wonder where Darlene found the jasper to stand with her?' Ken voiced the question. 'She couldn't have had enough money left after buying the chaise and horse to hire some wandering gun.'

'It don't make any difference,' Frank vowed. 'No one gets away with killing a Maitland. When we catch up with Darlene, we're going to put that man in a grave. He'd best enjoy life until we find him, because that's the day his life ends.'

* * *

The following day Nick and Darlene reached Lost Bow a little before noon.

They stopped the buggy at the livery stable and got their first look at Cy Bishop.

The man was on the long side of forty, thin enough to pass for a scarecrow, with more wrinkles in his face than a week-old shirt. He had sideburns that melded with a bewhiskered jaw. With a short beard and thick, bristled eyebrows, Kilpatrick thought it was like looking at an armpit with eyes.

Darlene explained who she was and Cy bobbed his head up and down.

'I read the news that Lex was killed in a hold-up attempt.'

'Yes,' Darlene admitted.

'But I had no idea my cousin had went and got himself a wife.' He didn't hide his surprise, pausing to inspect Darlene. 'You look a mite shy on years for an aged, devote gambler and gadabout like Lex.'

'I was rather desperate to get out of my situation,' Darlene admitted, turning to the buggy as Helen began to fuss.

'Jumpin' horny toads!' Cy exclaimed.

'You've got a little one too?' He clapped his hands in astonishment. 'Imagine that, Lex being someone's father. It's more than I can digest at one meal.'

'You seem to be the lady's only family.' Kilpatrick spoke up. 'And she has some trouble on her back trail.'

A matronly woman came out from the barn. She had obviously been tending to some of the horses as she had a currycomb in one hand. A smile of greeting brightened her unpretentious face.

'Who is our company, dear?' she asked Cy.

'A distant relative of mine,' he replied. 'You remember I told you about my cousin, Lex?'

There was an immediate coolness in the woman's expression. 'You mean the wild one in the family, the one who died with the price on his head?'

'This is his wife.' Cy gave a nod at Darlene, 'and her brand new baby.'

The woman tossed the currycomb aside and came forward. As Darlene took the baby in her arms, she moved close enough to peer down at Helen.

'I declare, she's a little darling!' the lady cried, her attitude changing instantly. 'And so tiny. She can't be more than a couple days old?'

'Yes,' Darlene told her. 'She arrived a little ahead of time. I had planned on being here in Lost Bow before she was born, but she had other ideas.'

'Is that a man's shirt she's wearing?'

Darlene flushed with embarrassment. 'I was going to get what I needed when I arrived.'

'And no blanket or proper-fitting diapers?'

'We used what we had,' Nick spoke up for Darlene. 'Does the general store carry the things we need for the baby?'

'I'm sure Mr Fargo has most everything,' Mrs Bishop replied. 'If not, I'll look around and find whatever else he doesn't have. We've four kids and I'm not much for throwing things away.'

'That would be a great help,' Darlene said.

The hostler scratched his chin. 'I just can't believe it . . . Lex, a family man. He was always about as windblown as a tumbleweed and claimed he never would put down roots.'

Darlene clarified. 'We were only married a little over a year. He died while attempting to rob a stage.'

'Yes, ma'am,' Cy replied. 'I saw the notice about his death with the last mail. His name was in the Denver paper obituaries.'

'I didn't know how to contact you, or if you were even still living here. I would have sent word myself.'

'That's OK,' Cy said. 'Even with my being his only kinfolk, we didn't really stay in touch. We ran around as kids together, but his father and mine went different directions. Last time I seen him was a dozen or so years ago, before I was married.'

'I'm sorry, Mr Bishop,' Darlene said softly. 'I shouldn't have come.' She ducked her head, looking down at Helen. 'It's just that I had no place else to go.'

'Worse yet,' Nick put in, 'the men who rode with her father want her back. I brung one of them along.'

'Landssakes!' Cy's wife cried, taking notice of the horses back of the carriage. 'Is that a body?'

'He didn't give me any choice, ma'am.'

Cy squinted at him and surmised: 'The fella strapped to the horse, you say he rode with Lex?'

'According to the lady here,' Nick replied.

'It's Josh Maitland,' Darlene informed Cy.

Cy grew serious. 'You know we don't have a lawman here in Lost Bow.' He snorted, a way of showing his disdain for the town. 'Shucks, there ain't but a dozen men living hereabouts. If I didn't manage a way station for the stage running north we'd have starved by now.'

'We would like to help,' his wife interposed, 'but we have four children between the ages of six and twelve. I don't see how we can be of any help against a gang of killers.'

Darlene sighed deeply. 'I'm sorry. I shouldn't have come.'

'Is there some place the lady can spend the night?' Nick asked the pair. 'I need to send off a couple telegrams and hope I can get answers back later tonight. Come morning, we'll be on our way.'

'Our way?' Darlene frowned at him. 'Where do you intend to take me?'

'I made a promise to your husband,' Nick replied. 'I'm going to get you and the baby to a safe place.'

'No such place exists, not from Maitland!'

'That's the way it has to be,' Nick retorted.

Darlene didn't know what to do. She was homeless, on the run, with a brand new baby to care for. She had no money and Lex's only kin had a wife and four kids. His family had to be his first priority. That meant she had no options, nowhere to go.

'I ought to surrender to them,' she said quietly. With an impassive look at Nick, 'I can't get away, and they will kill you if they catch us together.'

'She's got a point, sonny,' Cy spoke up. 'How are you going to take on all of Maitland's bunch?'

Nick didn't debate the issue. 'Like I said, I need to send off a couple of telegrams.' Turning to Cy, 'Is there any way to get this body taken care of here?'

'Fargo, over at the general store, does the burying — he's also the telegrapher.'

'Write me a note witnessing that this is Josh Maitland,' Nick said to Cy. 'I'll need it to collect the reward for Mrs Bishop.'

Darlene stared at him, mouth open, but no words forthcoming.

'Well, sure,' Cy told him. 'I can do that for you. And there's room for you in the loft. Feel free to toss your bedroll there for the night.'

Nick turned to Josh's horse, took the reins, and started walking toward Faro's general store.

'Man must think a heap of you, little lady,' Cy said to Darlene, not hiding a bit of envy. 'Five hundred dollars ought to set you up for a spell.'

'Let's go get what you need at the store, dear,' his wife invited Darlene. 'When we get back, I'll warm you a plate of that stew and get you a cool glass of lemonade. My eldest daughter can sleep with her sister so you will have her room on the back porch. It'll be more private for you and the baby that way.'

'You're more than generous,' Darlene said, and obediently followed Cy's wife as if in a trance. What kind of man was Nick Kilpatrick that he would risk his life and then fork over a huge bounty to her? Of course, their chance of escaping was nil, so she would likely never see any reward money.

Gato had been watching the road. He met Frank and the gang at the edge of town. He was surprised to see Frank leading a dozen men: nearly every member who had ridden with Maitland's Guerillas over the past several years. Facing the leader of the band, he hung his head in shame and remorse.

'I wasn't there when it happened,' he explained quietly. He told of how they had seen the buggy and lean-to on the side of the road and thought the horse might be near by. 'I was surprised when I heard a shot. I rode out of the brush in time to see some guy had just knocked Josh off his horse. I fired off a round at him, but he had cover and I was out in the open. I had to run or be killed too.'

'How can you be sure Josh was dead?' Dan asked.

'I got a good look — no doubt in my mind,' Gato replied. 'His eyes and mouth were wide open and blood had stained the front of his shirt. He was dead all right.'

'Will you know this guy if you see him again?' Frank wanted to know.

'You'll probably recognize him yourself,' Gato said. 'It was the same jasper who was riding guard on the stage when we were ambushed. He was wearing that black Stetson hat, the same kind Josh almost bought a few weeks back.'

'How did he get here and what's he doing with Darlene?' Dan asked in wonder.

'Darlene must have sent for him, asked him to meet her or something,' Skye guessed.

Ken was incredulous. 'You're saying she knew this guy and set us up for the ambush?'

'I don't know,' Skye admitted. 'But it sure seems strange, the very guy who was on the coach showing up to help Darlene.'

Frank snorted his contempt. 'I'll tell you what I think happened. Lex,' he swore vehemently, 'sold us out. He must have told that lawdog about our hideout.'

'That don't makes any sense,' Ken argued. 'If he was looking for us, how and why did the guy meet up with Darlene so far away from the ranch?'

'Maybe they were supposed to meet at Lost Bow,' Gato said, putting together pieces of the puzzle. 'It's the only thing that makes sense. Lex told her where to go if hc got caught or killed.'

'And he told this here lawman to meet her there.' Skye joined in with his logic. 'It all fits.'

'How far is it to Lost Bow?' Ken asked Gato, getting back to how to catch Darlene and her killer friend.

'Probably six hours or so if we take the main trail — the short cut saves about five miles,' he answered. 'It's too late to head that way today. The trail is hard enough to follow during daylight hours and your horses will need some rest.'

'Looks like we spend the night here.' Topper, one of the gang, spoke up for the first time. 'I could use a drink or two and a bed for the night.' He added gruffly, 'Always better to kill a man after a good night's sleep.'

'The gal and her gunnie pal will be running,' Ken said. 'Darlene knows we'll be after her, especially now that she is responsible for getting Josh killed.'

'They can't run fur enough,' Frank vowed. 'We will split up in the morning and make sure they don't reach Laramie.'

'They might go north,' Gato suggested.

Frank shook his head. 'No, they would be crossing endless miles of rugged country before they reached a decent-sized town in Montana. Their best chance is to try and reach Laramie, where there is law and the military near by to help them.'

'We'll need to cover both trails up to Lost Bow,' Ken pointed out. 'That way they can't backtrack on us.'

'Let's put up the horses,' Frank ordered, ending the dicussion. 'We'll get a few rooms and something to eat. Be ready to leave at first light.' He put a stern look on the group of men. 'That means no heavy drinking or gambling tonight for any of you.'

Gato skewed his face into a mask of hate. 'I won't be doing either of those things until I spit in the face of Josh's killer as he takes his last breath.'

10

Nick helped to bury Josh, paid for the chore and the goods that Darlene had purchased at the store, then ate a late meal at the only tavern in town. He returned to the livery after dark and found that Cy had put up his and Josh's horse, as well as Darlene's horse and buggy. He kicked a little straw together for a mattress, spread out his ground blanket for a bed and lay down. Before he could close his eyes he heard the sound of footsteps. He reached for his gun and sat up, ready for anything . . . or so he thought!

'It's me,' Darlene whispered, moving towards him as if she had the night vision of a puma.

He stared through the dark, able to make out her shadowy form as she closed in on where he'd made his bed. 'What are you doing out here in the barn?' he asked. 'I thought you and the baby were staying in the house?'

'Helen is asleep.'

He put his gun away as she knelt down next to where he was sitting. There was only a splinter of light coming from the Bishop house window, barely enough for him to see the outline of her features. He waited for her to speak her mind.

'I know you made a promise to Lex,' she began softly, 'but I want you to ride away. I don't wish to have you killed because of me.'

'And what about you? Do you simply go back with the Maitlands?' He grunted his opposition. 'Sorry, but I won't allow that.'

'Because of your promise to a dying man?' She made an unfeminine grunt of her own. 'Lex was a bandit, a thief, a man who would have killed you if he'd had the chance. You don't owe him anything.'

'This is about more than your dead husband.'

Darlene attacked with unveiled irritation. 'You're being a stubborn fool. Why do you want to risk throwing your life away?'

'Because I'm Helen's godfather,' Nick stated unequivocally. 'And I'm not going to let a bunch of robbers and murderers ruin the life of my godchild.'

She gasped with indignation. 'Godfather? I never asked you to be Helen's godfather.'

'You heard her cry out to me with her very first breath.'

Darlene frowned. 'What? You can't mean her little gasp and a couple of squeaks?'

'Well, those squeaks don't mean anything in English,' he countered. 'But in some Indian tongues, it was very close to the word for *daddy*.'

She harrumphed at the ridiculous notion. 'That's a load of rubbish!'

'Rubbish or not, Mrs Bishop, I reckon I at least earned the title of godfather. I helped bring your girl into this world. I tidied her up and wrapped her in my shirt. It was me who laid her in your arms. I even took on the chore to rinse her diapers and held her in my arms while you bathed and washed your clothes. I'm the closest thing Helen has to a father and I'll be hanged if I let you sacrifice both her life and your own.'

'You'll be worse than hanged!' Darlene retorted evocatively. 'Frank and his band of cutthroats will tear you into little pieces and feed you to the buzzards.'

'I've survived my share of battles,' he assured her.

'But . . . if I was to return with them, they might let you go.'

Nick remained firm. 'No, ma'am. You said Josh was the youngest of the Maitland boys, and Frank will hunt me until the day he dies. I reckon it's been decided: either I put him and the others in prison or I see them buried in the ground. That's the only way this can end.'

'Without me to slow you down, you

could leave this part of the country, go to California or Texas — some place where they can never find you.'

'Why would I do that?' he shot back. 'So I could lie awake at nights and pine about you and Helen? Think about what a miserable life the two of you have?'

'We're not your responsibility!'

'Beggin' your pardon, Mrs Bishop, but Helen *is* my responsibility.' He hesitated then added, 'So are you.'

Darlene went silent and stared at him in the dark. He was unable to see the look in her usually expressive brown eyes, but knew they were boring into him with a relentless scrutiny. For a full minute each of them remained poised, as if engaged in a battle of wills, each daring the other to blink.

'You are a stubborn man.' At last she broke the tension between them.

'When I know I'm doing what is right ... yes, ma'am; I'm as stubborn as a gray-back mule.'

Darlene sat back on her heels as if

indecisive, then rose to a standing position. She remained hovering over him for several seconds. Eventually a sigh of resignation escaped her lips. 'I'll say goodnight, Mr Kilpatrick,' she said softly.

'G'night, ma'am,' he reciprocated. She turned about and left the way she'd come, disappearing in the darkness.

Lying down again, Nick replayed the short encounter in his head. He could understand Darlene's not wanting to be responsible for his death. It showed she had decency and integrity. It was unfortunate that there hadn't been enough light to see the gal's face clearly. He wondered if Darlene's asking him to leave was all conscience, or was there another possibility?

She had offered to sacrifice herself and Helen so that he would not have to risk his life. Was it because the lady didn't want any more bloodshed on her account, or was there more to it than that? What if she was developing feelings for Nick?

Staring at the dark ceiling overhead, he considered that prospect. She was a new widow but had admitted she had not loved or respected her dead husband. He had not known Darlene very long, but he felt a strong bond with both her and the child. Whether she felt anything for him or not, he would see this through to the end.

* * *

JC arrived at the telegraph office and discovered a message waiting for him. It was cryptic, so it wouldn't mean much to anyone who happened to see the wire. He paused and read it aloud. 'Have wife. Family and friends following. Meet at Basque sheep camp in two days. Signed Nick.'

So Kilpatrick had the Bishop woman? That meant he had somehow managed to locate Lex's wife. Family and friends — obviously Maitland's gang, which could be a small army. The Basque sheep camp? He remembered Bob had mentioned something about that when they were on the trail of the bank robbers. The tracker knew Colorado and Wyoming like it was his own back yard. He would know where to go.

JC picked up a pencil and jotted down a message. As soon as the wire had been sent he went to get a meal and pick up some supplies. He had a feeling he would have a hard ride ahead.

★ ★ ★

To make it easier for Darlene to ride her horse Nick carried the baby, except for feedings. Helen slept most of the time, seemingly content with the natural rocking of his horse. A time or two she opened her eyes and appeared to study him. He wondered if she was curious as to whether he was her father or not. Of course, he doubted a new baby could see all that clearly for the first little while, so he expected Helen saw him as a blur, someone who spoke in a gentle voice and had her cradled in his arm.

He was glad she was a happy and quiet sort of baby, as a crying child could be heard a long way off. There shouldn't be anyone close, as he was avoiding the usual routes through the hills, making his way around cedars, dense undergrowth and sagebrush.

'We don't seem to be making very good time.' Darlene spoke up after a prolonged period of silence. 'If Frank and the others arrived in Lost Bow this morning, they could be coming after us already. We'll never get away from them.'

'The idea is not to get away clean. That's why Cy is going to tell them everything he knows. I didn't want him or his family to be hurt or killed for putting us up for the night.'

They had reached a small clearing, which allowed Darlene to come up alongside. She regarded him with a curious scowl.

'You want them to follow us? Is that your plan?'

'This is like playing checkers, ma'am. You set up your opponent with a move he doesn't expect in order to spring a trap. Maitland's Guerillas are going to be nothing but a memory when this is over.'

'Unless they tip over the checkerboard,' she declared. 'You can't possibly intend to take on Maitland and his men alone.'

'Where I'm leading them, there will be no escape.'

'No escape?' she lamented. 'For them or us?'

He offered her a crooked grin. 'Well, I'm hoping it's them.'

'Please tell me you have a detachment of soldiers from a nearby fort coming to help. If I had wanted for me and Helen to die at Maitland's hands, I would have stayed at their ranch and saved all of this running.'

Nick ignored her comments. 'Helen is starting to squirm some. I think she is getting hungry.'

'Yes, having such a small tummy, she

only goes about two hours between meals.'

'She's been eyeing me like she thinks I'm her father,' Nick said, unable to keep the pride from entering his voice.

Darlene snipped: 'With us likely to die in the next few hours, I suppose there's no harm in her thinking an utterly crazy man is her father.'

'Do you need for us to stop so you can get down and rest up a bit?'

'I don't think a few hours is going to make a difference. Does it really matter if we are killed this morning or this afternoon?'

Nick chuckled, but replied in a serious tone. 'Maitland and his bunch have been pushing their horses hard for the past couple of days, ma'am, while ours are well rested. We ought to be able to stay ahead of them until dark, then we will continue for another mile or so. They won't be able to follow our tracks so we will gain valuable time for our ride tomorrow.'

'What if they figure out where you're going?'

'No way they will guess that, not with the route I'm taking.'

They topped a hillock, from where the road between Rimrock and Laramie was visible below. Nick and Darlene both stopped their mounts, surprised to see a pair of sentries patrolling the trail.

'It's Boyd Fowler and Topper Rhodes, two men who sometimes ride with the Maitlands,' Darlene informed Nick. 'Now what?'

'Well, that tells us something,' Nick answered. 'Frank must have his whole gang involved in this hunt.'

'Remember what I told you, about Frank having twenty men?' Darlene said. 'How are you going to handle so many?'

'We took out six on the stage ambush,' he reminded her.

'Oh, that's different,' she said drily. 'I'm sure fourteen or fifteen men won't give you any trouble at all.'

Nick took a long look up and down

the trail below. If Frank had left two men posted near the short cut, he probably had a couple more at the main turn-off and another two or three would have ridden ahead to block the Laramie trail. Considering Frank was likely on their trail with a few more, Darlene's count could be about right. A dozen or more hardened killers would be quite a challenge.

'What do you know about the two men down there?' Nick asked.

Darlene did not hide her distaste. 'Scum of the earth. Lex told me Boyd shot a woman bank clerk one time for being slow to hand over the money, and Topper and a couple of his friends killed a family of eight Indians — some only children — just for the fun of it. I'll bet Frank called in every lowlife snake who ever rode with him.'

Nick recalled seeing Wanted posters on both the men who were guarding the trail. The dodger said they had committed rape, arson, murder and robbery. There would be a hangman's noose waiting for them, so they would go down fighting.

He and Darlene moved back out of sight and he climbed down with the baby. Darlene was not much of a horsewoman, but she did manage to get down on her own. She was ready when he passed Helen to her.

'I'll tie off your horse and you stay here and feed the baby. Once I've taken care of those two we will head south toward the railroad tracks. We'll make Frank guess we are either heading for Cheyenne or Laramie. Once it's dark, we'll turn south again and head for Colorado.'

'What if you get killed?' Darlene asked. 'Boyd and Topper are about as bad as any men you'll ever meet.'

'I've handled a few unsavory sorts before,' he offered her in reassurance. 'If there's shooting, it's likely Maitland's men will hear it and we'll have to pick up the pace.'

'You mean run like hell!' she exclaimed.

He raised his eyebrows. 'Never heard a proper lady swear before.'

'I've never felt like I was one step away from being killed before.'

'Hmm,' he said, showing her a grimace of displeasure. 'I'll let it pass this time, but don't be using bad language in front of our baby.'

Instead of firing back a heated reply, Darlene's grim demeanor gave way to a mirthless laugh. 'It won't happen again.'

11

'Traded a sixty-dollar buggy for a ten-dollar saddle?' Frank was livid. 'What kind of trade is that?'

Cy shook his shaggy head. 'Reckon they were in a hurry to get moving.'

'Which road did they take?'

'The fella didn't want to take the short cut or the main road either direction. He asked if there was a way through the hills that avoided all three.'

'And is there?'

'There's deer, elk and antelope about, mister,' Cy replied. 'Anywhere they travel makes a trail. I 'spect he turned south somewhere west of town.'

'Why did the two of them come to Lost Bow?' Dan asked.

'Lex Bishop was a cousin of mine.' Cy paused to spit a stream of tobacco juice into the dirt. 'But we wasn't close. I told that gal we didn't have no place for her and a baby.' He waved his arm towards the house. 'Shucks, I can't feed the wife and four kids I got now.'

'So they traded you a horse and left,' Frank deduced.

'That's about it,' Cy answered. 'However, the gent was toting a body along with him. He done had him buried in the local boneyard before they left.'

'Brother Josh,' Dan murmured sadly.

'What happened to his horse?' Ken asked Cy.

'Man left it here for you boys. He said he wasn't a horse-thief.'

'We don't need to be dragging along a spare horse,' Frank said. 'You tend him for us. If we don't come back in a week's time, he's yours.'

Cy grinned. 'I'll take you up on that offer.'

'Did the man contact anyone while he was here?' Ken wanted to know.

'I didn't ask and he didn't say,' Cy replied. 'I traded a saddle for the buggy and sent them on their way.' With a solemn look on his bewhiskered face, he said, 'Like I told you, I wasn't about to get involved in any trouble.'

Frank and his two brothers walked back over to where several of their men were waiting. All of them sat ready to ride, needing only a direction to go.

Gato was the most familiar with the area so he offered up a proposition. 'The road leading out of town ties into the main trail to Laramie about six miles from the fork where we came up. We've got men at both ends and a couple patrols watching in between.'

'What are you suggesting?' Frank wanted to know.

'If we follow the trail left by Darlene and her pal, we'll be a few hours behind.'

'Yeah, so?'

'I think we ought to send a rider to our men at both ends of the Lost Bow trail. Then,' Gato continued, 'the two groups could ride toward each other, watching the hills for any sign of our missing pair. We would all meet when we reached the main trail, but one bunch or the other might get lucky and cut off their escape.'

Ken endorsed the plan. 'That would also put us all in the same place so we could continue following the trail and not have to wait around for some of the men to catch up.'

'I like it,' Frank agreed. 'Send Red back down the main road to pick up those guys and Link ahead to get the others. The rest of us will pick up their trail and follow their tracks.'

'What about Josh?' Dan asked. 'Shouldn't we maybe say something over his grave?'

Frank snorted. 'Josh would likely pop up out of the ground and tell us to stop yapping and get after the worthless female and gunslick who caused his death!'

'Amen,' Ken agreed. 'Let's kick up some dust.'

★ ★ ★

Nick made a cautious approach, using the natural terrain to get close to the Maitland sentries. Concealed by the cedars and brush, he followed a gully or two until he was within a hundred feet of the two riders. With both men looking the other way, he drew his gun, then nudged his horse with his heels. She bounded up on to the road.

Unfortunately, these men made their living with a gun. Before he could order them to raise their hands, they both grabbed for their weapons. Darlene had said these were vicious killers; Nick had seen the Wanted notices and was also aware of how dangerous they were. He didn't hesitate: he fired at once. It should have given him the edge, but Topper and Boyd were seasoned veterans.

Nick scored a hit with his first round, but it was off the mark, burrowing a hole through Topper's right arm. Boyd fired back in an instant, the missile whistling past Nick's right ear.

Jumping his horse back and forth to

present a harder target, Nick advanced and pulled the trigger again, aiming at Boyd. The man was too quick, ducking low over his horse, causing him to miss. At the same time Topper joined the fray, using his left hand. He began blasting away wildly, as fast as he could pull the trigger.

Nick felt one round tear through his sleeve, then a sharp, white-hot pain burned along his left side. He kept his horse dancing zigzag and squeezed off a third shot. This one went true, catching Boyd in the motion of straightening up to take aim. The bullet struck the man's chest and knocked him off his horse.

Topper's gun clicked on empty and he spun his horse around to make a dash for safety. Nick jerked his mount to a stop, took careful aim, and put a slug between the outlaw's shoulders. Topper arched his back violently at the sudden entry of a scorching bullet. He swayed to one side, overcorrected trying to remain upright in the saddle, and spilled to the ground on the opposite side of his horse. He landed hard and rolled on to his face.

Nick took a quick look up and down the trail. The sound of gunshots carried a long way and some of Maitland's boys were probably close enough to have heard. With a cautious glance to ensure that neither gunman was capable of getting off another shot, Nick turned his steed, ready to ride back for Darlene and the baby.

To his surprise the lady was already riding down the last hill to join up with him. She had the baby tightly in one arm and a frightened look shone on her face.

'You're hit!' she cried, staring at the left side of his shirt.

Nick put his hand to the ribs on that side, a few inches below his armpit. He felt the wetness of the blood and pinned the palm of his left hand tightly against the wound to slow the bleeding.

'No time to check it right now. It doesn't feel too bad.'

'Your shirt is soaked with blood!'

Darlene said. 'We need to get that wound bandaged.'

'First, we've got to get off the trail,' Nick ordered. 'We need to get as far away as possible before the Maitland gang shows up.'

'Why didn't you shoot them from ambush?' she wanted to know. 'They were both hardened killers. What were you thinking, trying to get the drop on them?'

'I didn't want any shooting.' Nick excused his actions. 'We needed time to get ahead of the pursuit.'

'I hope the rest of your plan works better than this,' she told him critically. 'Even if you had tied them up, they would have rejoined the gang and helped to hunt us down.'

Nick disregarded the reproach and led the way down the road, searching for the best place to leave the trail with the least amount of tracks. With a lot of open country around, the first priority was to get out of sight.

'Do you need for me to carry Helen?'

he asked. 'We will have to ride hard for the next hour or two.'

'You keep pressure on your wound,' Darlene told him. 'I can manage Helen until we stop for a rest.'

Nick took a quick look at his side. 'The bleeding has about stopped. I think it's a graze and not very deep.'

'Better to be lucky than skillful in a gunfight, I suppose,' Darlene said.

Nick spied a run-off ditch, the bottom of which was lined with shale and rock.

'Here we go,' he said. 'Stay in the gully; it might hide our tracks for a little bit. We need every minute we can get.'

'I'll follow you, fearless leader,' Darlene quipped.

Nick glanced at her to see a wry smile on her lips. 'You're getting real comfortable around me, aren't you?' He gave a nod of satisfaction. 'That's a good sign.'

Rather than reply, she lifted one shoulder in a careless shrug.

'This way.' Nick turned to business.

Neck-reining his horse, he coaxed the mare to step carefully over a hearty clump of sage, then entered the rocky bottom of the wash. He led the way at an easy pace for the next fifty yards. Once the ditch bellied out into the flat country they put their horses into a lope. If one of Maitland's men arrived and spotted them, the hiding of their tracks would have been a waste of precious time.

★ ★ ★

Gato got down from his horse and surveyed the dusty tracks on the roadway. After checking the bodies and guns of Boyd and Topper he walked back and forth to read sign. After a bit he stopped and reported to Frank.

'The gunman with Darlene came from where we were following them.' He pointed at the brushy hillside. 'And the three of them shot it out. Boyd only got off a couple rounds, but Topper emptied his gun. There is a drop or two of blood over where the shooter was at, meaning one of them must have winged either him or his horse.'

'If it had been his horse he would have taken one of theirs,' Ken deduced.

'Unless he didn't know his mount had been hit.' Dan threw out a possible alternative.

Frank spoke through clenched teeth. 'Where did they go?'

'They started back along the trail to Rimrock, but their tracks are mixed in with Topper's and Boyd's. Those two were riding back and forth along here all morning. We know they didn't take the road east or west, because our boys came from both directions. I'll have to ride circle along the south side until I pick up their trail.'

'Get started,' Frank ordered. Then, turning to the others, 'A couple of you men help with the bodies. Drag them off of the road and cover them with rocks.'

As men moved to obey, Ken and Dan remained on their horses next to Frank.

Ken was first to speak. 'This *hombre* ain't no slouch with a gun, Frank. You think it's worth another couple of us getting killed to bring him down?'

'You heard what Gato said: the man is wounded. He's one man, with a woman and infant in tow. He can't have more than about an hour's head start and he won't dare try to make it to Rimrock. That leaves the railroad and a lot of open country between him and anywhere there might be a lawman.'

'I'm just saying: he's killed three of our number and we ain't set eyes on him yet.'

Frank snarled his reply. 'Gato says it's the same man who was guarding the stage. That means he helped with the killing of Lex and the other boys. We've got a major grudge to settle with that man.'

'He took Topper and Boyd.' Dan voiced his concern. 'That's some pretty fair shooting.'

'The guy came out of the brush ready to fight. Topper and Boyd were taken by surprise.' Frank stared aimlessly off in a southerly direction and muttered an oath. 'We'll get them. We'll get them both.'

Ken and Dan exchanged looks. They had never stood up to Frank and this would be no different. Regardless of the fate awaiting them, they would ride at his side.

12

The rolling hills were a welcome sight. After a mile or two Nick made a sharp turn toward Laramie. They rode for another hour and then stopped near a natural basin where there was a little water from the last rain. It wasn't something they could drink, but tracks visible along the edge showed that deer and other animals had visited the pool recently.

While the horses drank and grazed at the few patches of buffalo grass, Darlene put the baby down. She was a mother now and the sense of responsibility entered her personality.

'Sit down and take off your shirt,' she instructed Nick. 'I have a piece of cloth Cy's wife gave me. I was going to try and make a second nightgown for Helen, but I'll tear it into a strip and it will work as a bandage.'

Nick did as he was told and carefully pulled the material away from the wound. He had rightly assessed that it was only a graze; a two-inch furrow left by a bullet passing mere inches from his heart was revealed.

Darlene cleaned the area with a little water from the canteen and tore the cloth into a narrow strip. She started to wrap the wound, but Nick noticed her hesitate when she was forced to lean close to him. As she reached around and encircled his chest, he felt her breath on his neck and shoulder. She seemed uncomfortable rubbing up against him and her face was flushed by the time she tied the material in place.

'Done like a professional medico.' Nick praised her handiwork, pretending not to have noticed her discomfiture.

'Yes, well . . . ' but she didn't finish. Instead, she provided him with his extra shirt. It was no longer needed as a nightdress for the baby and she had laundered it the previous night. As he put on the shirt and began to tuck in the garment, Darlene sat down at his side.

'We can't be very far ahead of Frank and the others,' she said, the fear evident in the expression on her face.

'There's an old trick I learned from chasing Indians,' Nick informed her. 'Only let the enemy get a glimpse of you when you're out of rifle range. The army would often chase a band of warriors for months at a time and never get close enough to shoot at them. Had the Indians taken up arms and stood to fight against the soldiers, they would have been annihilated in a few months. Instead, the war has dragged on for years and is still going strong in some parts of the country.'

'So we're pretending to be the Indians here?'

He grinned. 'Trust me, ma'am, I won't let anyone harm you or our child.'

Darlene's brows drew into a tight knot with her scowl. 'That's twice you have called Helen *our* child.'

'I helped to bring her into this world. I'm the only father she knows.'

'But you're not her father.'

Nick looked upon the sleeping infant. Her lash-adorned eyes were closed and a mere sprinkle of dark hair covered her perfectly formed head. She had a tiny button nose, a cupid's bow mouth and ears as delicately molded as seashells.

'It might seem impossible to you, ma'am,' he said gently, 'but I love little Helen, as certain as if she were my own blood.'

'You . . . ' Darlene coughed. 'You love my daughter?'

'Yes, ma'am, I do,' Nick admitted. 'And I think you ought seriously to consider me to be the man who takes on the duties of being her father . . . and your husband.'

The woman was visibly struck dumb. She stared at Nick as if he had been chewing on loco weed.

'That is,' he added, seeking to clarify his position, 'unless you prefer to look for another man like Lex Bishop.'

'I .. I ... ' She had to clear her throat. 'No! I mean, Lex turned out to be nothing like I thought he would be. He was handsome and knew how to flatter a girl. I was gullible, lonely, and tired of working endlessly at my aunt's laundry. I married him to escape a horrid existence and it turned out to be the biggest mistake of my life.'

'There you are!' Nick stated confidently. 'Lex was smooth as silk, while I'm more rough and durable, kind of like burlap. He was handsome, whilst I ain't never had to fight off women admirers. Then he was a gambler and drinking man, and I've never indulged in either of those vices.' Nick shook his head. 'Plus, I'll bet he wasn't all that happy about becoming a father, while I'm ready, willing and eager to take on the chore.'

'What about me and *my* feelings?' Darlene wanted to know. 'You still call me *ma'am*. You've never even tried to hold my hand or ... ' The flush returned to her cheeks, but she finished meekly, 'or flirt with me.'

'You are a recent widow and new mommy. I didn't figure it was proper to commence courting yet.'

'But this is OK?' she cried. 'You're asking to be the father of a child, without ever trying to woo the mother!'

Nick put his arm around her shoulders, rewarded at once that she did not object. 'It isn't that I haven't thought about holding you close,' he told her seriously. 'And I admit, I believe that a kiss from your tempting lips would equal whatever heaven is like.' He uttered a sigh and went on. 'I might not have the slick-talking ways of a man like Lex Bishop, but I think you're the sweetest, most beautiful woman on earth, and I get an ache in my heart every time I look at you.'

'Maybe the pain is from something you ate,' Darlene snipped coyly.

Ever so gently he leaned down and touched his lips to her own. She didn't resist and he didn't linger, preferring to make a point rather than incite a passionate response. Pulling back at once, he said, 'I'm not asking you to make a lifelong commitment right this minute. I'll give you time to think it over.'

Darlene laughed and displayed a pixie simper. 'Do you really think that's a good idea? What if the Maitland gang kill you before I get a chance to answer yes or no?'

'I figured I might have earned your trust by now,' Nick retorted. 'I promised to take care of you and Helen and I'm a man of my word.'

'Yes,' she was quick to emphasize, 'but that was before you got yourself shot too.'

'I'll duck a little quicker next time,' he promised.

'All right, Mr Kilpatrick. If we're both still alive tomorrow night,' she issued the condition, 'I'll give you my answer.'

'I prefer Nick,' he said.

'All right, *Nick*,' she corrected. 'And, now that you've kissed me, you ought to start calling me Darlene.'

'It would be an honor, Darlene,' Nick said, smiling broadly. 'Reckon we best get going; we need to put some miles behind us.'

★ ★ ★

The animals were stopped for a rest. Frank stood alone and stared out over the open country ahead. He thought about Josh, the youngest member of the family, the brother he had raised like a son. He blinked back tears of grief and broke his perusal as Ken came up to stand next to him.

'They're still headed for the railroad tracks. They might be able to board a train before we catch up to them.'

'We checked the train schedule when we started after Darlene,' Frank told him. 'There isn't a train due through this part of the country going either way until the day after tomorrow.' He rubbed his chin and remained pensive. 'No, our gunman must have something in mind, perhaps following the tracks west to Laramie or east to Cheyenne.'

'You seen the shirt he left behind. It was pretty well soaked with blood. Maybe Darlene is the one doing the guiding?'

'The footprints show the man got on his own horse. He must not be in too bad a shape.'

'Not a town or major ranch for fifty miles in any direction from here,' Ken remarked. 'If he doesn't turn at railroad tracks, then where could he be going?'

'He might be trying to cut across country and reach Fort Collins.' Gato's voice caused both men to turn and look at him. He had obviously been listening.

'There's a lot of hard country between here and Fort Collins,' Ken said.

Frank removed his worn hat and fanned his face. It wasn't hot, but it was warm and he was sweating some. 'It's a possibility,' he replied to Gato, 'but we aren't going to split up until we know for sure what he's doing.'

'He's been resting more than he would if he was alone,' Gato informed the two brothers. 'It could be from his wound, but more likely he is taking it easy on Darlene and the baby.'

'They're on fresher horses,' Ken reminded them. 'And they can ride after dark and maybe change direction on us.'

'We'll stop at a grassy spot as soon as it gets too dark to see his trail.' Frank summarized his intentions. 'Each man will water and rub down his steed. We'll eat a good meal, get what sleep we can, and be on the move at daylight. Tomorrow, we're going to run our mounts into the ground. No matter what Darlene's destination, there's no town of any size that they can reach tomorrow. If we ride like a herd of stampeding cattle, we can run him down before dusk.'

'That ought to work,' Ken agreed. 'He won't expect us to risk losing them altogether by giving our horses one hard push.'

'Let's keep moving. We need to get as close as possible before darkness sets in.'

* * *

Nick changed direction after dark and didn't stop for two hours. Helen was fussing by the time he tethered the horses for the night and set up a cold camp. Darlene, who hadn't been eating all that well, didn't have enough milk to satisfy the hungry infant. As she cuddled and attempted to soothe the baby, Nick dug into his supply sack and removed a tin of Borden's condensed milk. Cy's wife had provided them with a baby bottle, so he mixed two parts water and one part milk.

'Where did you learn about that?' Darlene wanted to know, watching as he shook the container to mix the liquids thoroughly.

'Back when we were chasing after

Indians, we always carried a couple tins of milk. A time or two we found a baby that had been hidden or abandoned after a raid. With the mother missing or dead, we needed a way to feed the little tykes.'

Darlene had to coax Helen to take the bottle, but she eventually decided it was either the mix of milk and water or go hungry. She cooperated and was soon asleep with a full tummy.

'Great invention, milk in a can,' Darlene said, carefully laying Helen down.

'A storekeeper told me the guy, Borden, was on a sea voyage, returning from the London Great Exhibition of '51, where he had won some kind of award for his meat biscuit in a tin. The two cows on board ship got sick and couldn't produce milk and he had to watch infants go hungry. At least one of them died. He decided then and there to figure a way to provide a condensed milk that could be stored until needed.'

Darlene studied him in the darkness.

'You are more than the simple lawman you pretend.'

'I don't know that I've been pretending,' Nick replied. 'Ever since the War Between the States, I've been leading a group of men called rangers. After the Rebs, it was Indians, then bandits. Hunting and fighting is all I've done since I left home at eighteen.'

'If that's so, exactly what kind of life are you offering me and Helen?' she queried. 'I don't fancy staying at home waiting for a husband to come back between hunting campaigns, any more than I did sitting at home waiting for a man who was out robbing people.'

'I've gotten to know a few men running express companies. Along with a couple of the men I've been working with, I aim to start up an express outfit . . . probably over on the western slope of Colorado. The Ute Indians are friendly and the farmers there raise a good deal of produce. With no train for shipping, they can use a good freight and transport company.'

'So you'd be off driving a wagon and making deliveries?'

'Not me. I'll be running the office and home every night after work.'

She smiled. 'You have all the answers, don't you?'

'All but the one I asked you for,' he reminded her.

She lay down on the ground blanket next to Helen. He thought she wasn't going to reply, but she ultimately murmured, 'We haven't made good our escape yet.'

Nick accepted the answer and moved off into the dark. He walked back in the direction they had come. Having selected a natural hollow between two hills for their camp, he climbed to the top of the higher hillock and was able to see quite a distance. There were no fires visible, no torches dancing in the blackness to indicate the outlaws were trying to follow their tracks. Maitland and his men had likely given up for the night. All the same, he picked out a spot just below the summit and sat down to keep watch. He could doze a little at a time and yet remain on guard. It would get him by this one night.

* * *

Frank let Gato, who knew horses better than anyone else in the gang, set the pace. Gato was also the best tracker and, once they found Darlene and her pal's campsite, the trail was easy to follow. They rode hard, ate in the saddle and walked the horses a few minutes each time they became winded. With such a relentless and furious pursuit, they drew ever closer to their prey.

'Looks like fresh droppings!' Gato reported a little after noon, holding up his hand to stop the gang. He jumped down and quickly tested the horse-leavings. 'Not even an hour,' he said, displaying a grin. 'We have closed the distance to a mile, possibly a little more.'

'How fast are they traveling?' Ken asked Gato.

'Looks to be a steady walk. If they don't see our dust we ought to catch them long before the sun goes down.'

'Let's keep up the pace,' Frank ordered. 'We should be close enough to see them pretty soon.'

'Need to save a little of our horses' strength for the final push,' Gato suggested. 'Once they spot us they'll make a run for it. We won't be able to catch them if our animals are completely spent.'

'Looks like a small mountain range yonder,' Skye observed, pointing off in the direction they were headed. 'We might be able to circle or cut them off once we reach the lower hills.'

'I recollect there's a box canyon over that way,' Gato said. 'There used to be a sheep camp where the herder kept his sheep during bad weather.'

'Some call it Dead Man's Canyon,' one of the others chimed in. 'It earned the name after a couple of prospectors got trapped there and killed by Indians back in '65.'

'It's a good place for them to spend the night,' Gato said. 'There's some natural pools for water and an old Indian cave at the far end of the gorge.'

'That's where he's headed!' Frank declared. 'He is going to spend the night there.'

'The guy won't enter the canyon if he sees our dust,' Skye pointed out.

Gato remounted his horse and looked at Frank. 'If we split into three groups, we can force him into the box canyon. Once inside, there's no escape. We'll have them trapped.'

Frank took his advice. 'Skye, you take three men and veer off about a half-mile to the left. Ken, you take three more and do the same on the right. Get ahead of them or cut them off and make sure they don't go around the canyon. We'll push from behind and all of us will meet at the entrance to Dead Man.' He snorted confidently. 'We'll give people a second reason to call it Dead Man's Canyon!'

13

The sun was sinking in the western sky and the mouth to Dead Man was a mile in the distance when Nick spotted riders coming from their left flank. Even as he looked over his shoulder, he saw the dust of more riders closing in from behind them.

'Over there!' Darlene called out, pointing to their right flank. 'Four men on horseback!'

Nick tucked Helen tightly into the crook of his arm, gauged how close they were and shouted, 'Let's go!' He kicked his horse into a run and Darlene did the same, staying right at his side.

After a short way, Nick turned his head and shouted to Darlene: 'Soon as we reach the opening to the canyon, you take Helen and ride to the cave. It's not more than a half-mile. You wait there until I come for you.'

The fear and uncertainty showed clearly on Darlene's face, but she gave a nod of understanding.

Nick let the horses run wide open, knowing it would mean death or capture if Maitland managed to block him from getting inside the canyon. He remembered the mouth was narrow, no more than a couple hundred feet across. To either side were sloping crags where a man could seek cover and slow the pursuit. However, he knew he couldn't stop a dozen men on his own.

The riders from both flanks and those behind converged, but, from what Nick could tell, their horses were laboring near exhaustion. The gang had obviously run their mounts long and hard to get this close.

The canyon loomed ahead, looking like nothing more than a small gap or defile between two hills. Once through the entrance the walls rose suddenly and the half-mile basin was a cirque, ringed by an impassable escarpment. A person might climb up the rocky precipice to get out, but a horse or other live-stock would be trapped on the valley floor.

Riding full out, Nick and Darlene gained a couple hundred yards' advantage from Maitland and his men. They didn't slow down until they reached the gateway to the canyon. Then he pulled back on the reins. Darlene did the same and he passed her the baby.

'Nick,' she gasped, out of breath from the hard ride, 'you can't hold them off by yourself. You'll be killed!'

He flashed her a confident smile. 'Sounds downright natural, you calling me by my first name. I'd say you're becoming fond of me.'

Her expression was something between horrified and astonished. 'Really?' she cried. 'There are a dozen men closing in on us and now you're flirting?'

'Might not be much time later,' he said. 'Have you made up your mind about me?'

'Yes,' she declared. 'You are definitely crazy!'

Nick took a glance over his shoulder. Maitland's gang was seconds away. 'Get going — clear to the end! The cave is to the right side, at the base of the cliff. Wait for me.'

Darlene appeared anxious to say something more, but there was no time. She cradled Helen in her arm and quickly leaned from her saddle. Nick was only about half-prepared, but he managed to react in time to meet her halfway for a short but heartfelt kiss.

'Be careful!' Darlene pleaded softly. Then she kicked her horse into a lope, hurrying to get out of harm's way.

Nick was consumed in a blissful haze as he turned his mount about and sat facing the approaching riders. The sight of a dozen men bearing down on him, prepared and eager to kill him, sobered him immediately.

'Come on,' he challenged them fervently. 'I'm going to defend my woman and child. You lowlife scum didn't bring near enough men to take them away from me.'

A large, older man was out in front, waving his arm and apparently giving orders: probably Frank Maitland. The others were armed, brandishing either a rifle or a pistol as they closed the distance between themselves and Nick.

Having been involved in numerous skirmishes over the past ten years, Nick knew exactly when an enemy was in range. Even as they began shooting at him he chambered a round into his Winchester, took aim and waited.

The bandits spread out, mounting a ragged, cavalry-type charge. Bullets were thudding into the earth and dust was kicked up a hundred feet out in front of Nick. He picked one man who was riding a little more erect than the others, allowed for the breeze, distance and maximum range, then squeezed the trigger.

The target disappeared in the dust from the other men's horses. One saddle was empty, but the entire gang had come into range. Nick whirled his horse about and headed deeper into the canyon. There was adequate cover all around, including an outcrop of boulders to either side, but he kept riding until he was a hundred yards from the cave entrance. Reining his horse in behind an elevated mound of rock and dirt, he jumped to the ground, took cover behind a large boulder, and aligned his sights for another shot.

The eleven horsemen entered the mouth of the canyon and quickly broke off from their frontal attack, attempting to flank Nick's position. Their idea was to approach Nick from several sides and fill him with enough lead to fill a wheelbarrow.

Suddenly three other rifles opened fire — two from the bandits' left and one from the right side of the basin. Maitland's gang was caught in a deadly crossfire. A pair of gunmen were knocked from their mounts, while the other riders began racing about, impotently throwing shots at the trio of phantoms in the rocks while seeking cover.

Nick knocked a second man out of his saddle and the three expert shooters downed another man each.

The man whom Nick assumed to be Frank waved his arm and yelled for everyone to retreat. He led the way, making a run for the outlet of the narrow pass. Most of the raiders followed his order, making their retreat.

Then two more rifles opened up, blasting away in rapid fire, one from either side of the gap entrance.

Several outlaws yanked their mounts to a stop. Spinning about on dancing horses, they were trapped in the open, with no cover or protection from the half-dozen sharpshooting riflemen. The fight sounded like a war, with panic-stricken men scrambling for safety, wounded men crying out, and gunfire exploding to shatter the late-afternoon calm. Unable to find targets, the outlaws' return shots screamed harmlessly off the protective wall of rocks. With the exception of JC, Nick's rangers were seasoned veterans. They continued the barrage, wounding or killing the few bandits who dismounted and sought cover behind rocks or clumps of brush. Others remained mounted and raced in a circle, seeking a safe haven from the deadly flying lead.

At last it became obvious to the remaining outlaws that they were in a no-win situation. One by one they began to throw down their guns and raise their hands. The remaining two or three who refused to give up were quickly dispatched by the accurate shooters in the rocks. Nick spotted Frank Maitland, slumped forward over his mount, arms dangling uselessly along the horse's neck. Lacking guidance, the animal came to an uncertain stop. It was standing still when he fell to the ground.

Gus, Bob and JC appeared from behind their cover, while the Simmons brothers showed themselves at the canyon entrance. When the smoke cleared, five bandits had surrendered with only minor injuries, while two of the wounded were on death's doorstep. The rest had died during the heated skirmish.

Bob and the Simmons boys took charge of the prisoners. JC flashed a wide grin as he came over to meet up with Nick.

'We only arrived about an hour before you got here,' he said. 'Good thing Bob knew this is where you wanted to meet.'

Nick laughed, relieved to have survived and that none of his ranger pals had been hurt. It had been a successful trap. 'I'm glad you were able to get all of the boys here in time to save my hide.'

Gus, after checking on the prisoners, came over to join them. He reported the status of the Maitland gang. 'A couple of these jaspers claimed to be only cattle rustlers, Captain. They swear they never robbed any payrolls or killed anyone. The one Maitland — Ken, he said his name was — he vouched for the pair before he died.'

'Any of the Maitland boys survive?'

'No, Ken was the last. Also, the two bandits who were in on the ambush of the coach — Skye and Gato — they are both done for, too.'

'It'll be dark soon,' Nick said. 'See to the wounded and round up all of the horses. We'll take the whole bunch to Fort Collins tomorrow.'

'We'll set up camp next to the water hole,' Gus proposed. 'You and the lady can stay at the cave and have a little privacy that way.'

'Privacy?' JC chirped. 'Why does Kilpatrick need any privacy?'

Gus stared at Nick and shook his head. 'You sure you want to keep someone around as dense as this here youngster?'

'Oh!' JC exclaimed, a dim light dawning within his brain. 'You're saying our brave leader has a hankering for the Bishop woman?'

'Is you blind as well as dumb?' Gus snorted. 'Didn't you see that goodbye betwixt the gal and the captain at the canyon entrance?'

'The kiss?' JC appeared mystified. 'A little ol' kiss don't mean nothing.'

Nick scowled at him. 'Perhaps you've forgotten the day we met. It was a *little ol' kiss* that about got your hide peeled with a bullwhip.'

JC grinned. 'Well, I reckon a kiss means whatever you and the woman involved agree upon.'

'Yonder is mother and child,' Gus told Nick, nodding to the head of the canyon where Darlene had come from her hiding-place. 'Was I you, I wouldn't stand here talking to us. A woman likes to think she's special, that she comes first.'

'Words of wisdom from an old married man,' JC said. 'G'wan. Take care of your new family, boss. We got this covered.'

Nick picked up his horse and rode the remainder of the way to the cave. As Gus had discerned, Darlene and the baby were waiting for him. He stopped a few feet from her to dismount. Before his foot touched the ground, Darlene launched a verbal attack at him.

'Fine thing,' she grated the words harshly. 'You let me think you were going to take on the Maitlands' gang all by yourself!'

Nick rotated about to face her. 'I didn't know if JC had gotten my telegram,' he tried to explain.

'Don't give me that!' She was still breathing fire. 'You honey-duped me into kissing you. I thought you might die defending me and Helen.'

'I was prepared to do whatever I had to do,' he assured her.

Darlene didn't back-pedal. 'How were you going to protect us when you were dead?'

Her raising her voice caused Helen to begin to cry. Nick reached out and took the baby from her arms. He spoke soft and gentle to Helen and she quieted right down. He then met Darlene's ire with a bit of a smirk.

'Smart little girl we have here,' he said. 'You can see that she has accepted me as her father. Now, do you want to continue to be angry and cause distress to our baby, or are you going to come over here and let me hold you both in my arms?'

The heat abated from Darlene's cheeks. After a short hesitation she stepped over close enough for Nick to encircle her with his free arm and pull her close.

'I apologize for not telling you about the plan, but I had no way of knowing if JC got my message. If he and the others hadn't shown up, I would have had to fight my way back to the cave and make a stand here.'

She studied his face for a moment. 'You really didn't know?'

'I sent wires to each telegraph station along his route, but we had to leave before I got an answer back. I don't know if he even took time to wire me a reply.'

Darlene lifted her chin and looked up at him. 'Then you aren't making idle boasts. You really were ready to take on the Maitland gang by yourself?'

'We didn't have a lot of choices. There's no way we could have stayed ahead of them long enough to reach Fort Collins. And I'd have had no chance against them out in the open. This was our best chance . . . and it worked out fine.'

'Under the circumstances, I suppose I can forgive you for deceiving me.'

'As you can see, Helen has already done that.' He looked down at the baby's tiny, beautiful face. 'What about you? Are you going to break our little girl's heart by not marrying her father?'

'You promise to make us a home and not go running after every outlaw or renegade Indian you hear about?'

'With the reward money for all of these characters, we will be able to open the express office and start making a good living.' He tipped his head in the direction of his rangers. 'And we've got a full crew of men ready to go to work. Gus, being the only married man, will run the stable and work with me at the office.'

'All right.' Darlene sighed dreamily. 'But I need you to do one more thing before I give you my answer.'

Nick was not slow to act this time. He leaned down and kissed the mother of their child. When she responded, the warmth of her lips told him he'd done exactly what she wanted him to do. He had her answer; they were going to be a family.

We do hope that you have enjoyed reading this large print book.

Did you know that all of our titles are available for purchase?

We publish a wide range of high quality large print books including:
Romances, Mysteries, Classics
General Fiction
Non Fiction and Westerns

Special interest titles available in large print are:
The Little Oxford Dictionary
Music Book, Song Book
Hymn Book, Service Book

Also available from us courtesy of Oxford University Press:
Young Readers' Dictionary
(large print edition)
Young Readers' Thesaurus
(large print edition)

For further information or a free brochure, please contact us at:
Ulverscroft Large Print Books Ltd.,
The Green, Bradgate Road, Anstey,
Leicester, LE7 7FU, England.
Tel: (00 44) **0116 236 4325**
Fax: (00 44) **0116 234 0205**

DARK MESA

Hank J. Kirby

Ross McCall is a rounder-up of maverick cattle for his own small herd. When he provides aid to wounded bandit Ace Morgan — last surviving member of an outlaw gang, and his pa's old comrade — the dying man repays his kindness by sharing the location of the band's last haul, hastily squirrelled away on McCall's land. But others are after the loot, imprisoning McCall and searching his his spread for the money. On his release, can McCall face down those who would snap up his land — and succeed in finding his legacy?